Austin City Blue

Austin City Blue

Jan Grape

Five Star • Waterville, Maine

This novel is a work of fiction. Names, characters, places and incidents are either the product of the author's imagination, or, if real, used fictitiously.

Five Star First Edition Mystery Series.

Published in 2001 in conjunction with Tekno-Books and Ed Gorman.

Cover photo courtesy of The Austin Convention and Visitors Bureau.

Set in 11 pt. Plantin by Myrna S. Raven.

Printed in the United States on permanent paper.

Library of Congress Cataloging-in-Publication Data

Grape, Jan.
    Austin City blue / Jan Grape.
        p.   cm. (Five Star first edition mystery series)
      ISBN 0-7862-3014-2 (hc : alk. paper)
      1. Police — Texas — Austin — Fiction. 2. Austin (Tex.)
— Fiction. 3. Policewomen — Fiction. I. Title.
II. Series.
PS3607.R425 A87 2001
    813'.6—dc21   2001042855

For Elmer
who never gets upset when I go to another world
for days on end.
In memory of my dad, Tom Barrow,
who handed me the first mystery
which began my affair with the genre.
and in memory of my mom, Pee Wee Pierce.

Acknowledgments

It's impossible to thank everyone who gives of their valuable time and expertise in order to make the words ring true, but this book absolutely would not have been possible without the expert assistance and support of Officer Lianne Crowe (formerly of the R.O.P. Unit of APD now retired); Jan Hull, (former Communications Supervisor, APD); Commander Shauna Jacobson, head of the Training Division of the Austin Police Academy, teachers and alumni of Austin Citizen's Police Academy. To Detective Linda Cooper, Forgery Unit of APD, the former director of Ops at Austin Citizens Police Academy who made the introductions to fellow officers, then read and critiqued this manuscript for APD accuracy. I'm honored to know each of you. To Mike Meredith of the Potter County District Attorney's Office who gave expert legal advice on sentencing and parole violations. To Kate Stine for expert editorial advice. To Robert J. Randisi who gave me the title. Also I couldn't have done it without the push, comments, critique, and encouragement of the Black Shoes—Barbara Smith, Jeff Abbott and Susan Cooper—hey thanks, guys. To Ed Gorman, Marcia Muller and Carol Lea Benjamin who pushed, pulled, prodded, harangued and encouraged whenever I lagged. To Sue Grafton who read and offered encouragement. To Nancy Bell who did final read for errors. To Elmer Grape who gave constant support and encouragement, who never let me give up, and whose love makes me complete. Any errors herein are mine and should not reflect or detract in any way on the Austin Police Department or others who gave so freely of their advice and help.

Early one morning (in the 1880s) a large pool of blood was found near Fifth and Congress Avenue giving the impression to passers-by that some dark and dreadful tragedy had been enacted there but nothing was ever learned concerning it. (Compiled from: Austin History Center Records.)

Chapter 1

I looked at myself in the women's locker room mirror, surprised to see I didn't look any different. Yes, my hair looked windblown and my eyes somewhat bloodshot and fatigue lines radiated from each corner, but that was all. Totally normal. I didn't know what I expected. A gray streak, maybe, suddenly appearing in my hair? A scarlet *K* on my forehead? The mirror's reflection didn't show anything unusual, but I whispered, "I am a killer."

I'd never killed anyone before and I hope I never will again.

The victim? A young male. In death, he looked no more than eighteen, but I now knew he was twenty-five. I remember how his black hair swept back from his thin face and how his black eyes stared in that glassy way of the dead. That tragedy left one reality quite strong—that pool of blood staining the concrete is forever etched in my mind.

Pure and simple self-defense? Yes, indeed. And in a way, you could say I have a license to kill. I'm a police officer for the Austin Police Department. The shoot was perfectly legal by anyone's standards.

I didn't know who he was when I shot him. How could I? He was only a shadowy figure in the darkness. I saw him force a female officer he'd already wounded to walk ahead of him; her hand dripped her life force. He had used her for a shield. The guy *had* asked for it, hadn't he?

In the last few minutes of his life before I arrived on the scene, and before taking this officer hostage, he had shot another policeman, a man named Lopez, one of the new young ones.

When I'd confronted the suspect I had identified myself as a police officer. I'd asked him to give it up, but he shoved the policewoman to the floor and fired at me. That was when I shot him.

Only afterwards, when it was over, did I find out he was Jesse Garcia—a felony suspect—wanted for eight long months because of an earlier shooting. Wanted for shooting yet another APD officer.

For the past eight months, that other officer lay in a coma in a nursing home with little hope of recovery while his shooter, Jesse Garcia, was hiding in Mexico. I could picture Garcia drinking tequila and chasing girls.

That other officer? Formerly a Special Missions officer. Formerly handsome, witty, intelligent, funny, gentle. Formerly a loving husband. Byron Barrow, *my* husband.

Physical evidence proved without a doubt that Garcia, a known gang-banger, had fired the gun that wounded Byron, but Garcia took off on the morning the arrest warrant had been issued. Ran to Mexico.

"Zoe?" Lynda Haynes, a civilian working desk duty at headquarters, stuck her head inside the restroom door. "Are you okay, Zoey?"

I hated being called Zoey because my name is pronounced Zoe like Joe. But Lynda's tone was gentle, and I knew she only meant it in an endearing way. She wore a heavy perfume that wafted ahead, filling my nostrils and causing my stomach to churn in rebellion. I barely managed to keep it in control. She came inside, stood next to the sink, and stared at my reflection briefly before looking at me.

Was she also searching for a scarlet *K*?

"You been throwing up?" she asked.

She wasn't accusing in any way, her only concern was how I felt, how I was dealing with the aftermath—nothing more.

"I don't think there's anything left down there."

"Yeah. I figured." She reached out and patted my forearm. "Rob Morton wanted me to check on you."

"Tell him I'll be out in a few minutes."

"If it makes you feel any better, Zoe, that puke got what he deserved." Her lips stretched into a brief smile before she turned and walked out.

Turning on the cold water faucet, I pulled a handful of paper towels from the dispenser and wet them. I held the cool wadded towels against my eyes then rewet them and wiped my mouth. I found a comb in my shoulder bag, ran it through my hair, put a dab of color on my lips and looked in the mirror once more. "That's a little better, Zoe."

Do I have regrets? Yes—and no. I'll never forget that bloody horror and the knowledge that I took the life of another human being, but I'll also never forget that I got the scumbag who nearly destroyed my life eight long months ago.

In 1861, in the midst of a grove of oaks and elms only three miles north of the state capitol and seat of the state government, sat a gray limestone building that was first known as the state lunatic asylum. It was later named Austin State Hospital and was the first known in Texas to care for and treat mentally ill. (Compiled from: Austin History Center Records.)

Chapter 2

I knew how the department's mandatory procedures take over when a police officer fires his weapon, but it had been years since I'd seen it up close and personal. I suspect the procedures are much the same in any metropolitan department. A debriefing session is held almost immediately with the officer-involved-in-a-shooting investigators. An awkward sounding title, but that's what they're called in our town. Homicide is also called and after a preliminary statement at the scene you are hustled to police headquarters and questioned.

The media is there but not allowed to get to you then. They are yelling questions but they're not sure if you're a victim or witness or what and, besides, the police public information office will handle them.

Once downtown the homicide investigators asked their questions and I answered and they asked questions of my answers and they asked questions of my questions. Eventually, I made a formal statement and signed it. The Internal Affairs Department (we call them I.A.) sessions would wait at least until tomorrow. It was after midnight and I wanted to go home and pull the covers over my head to keep the monsters away but now I *had* to talk to the police psychologist. It was mandatory. Although it could have waited until morning, our psychologist happened to be on duty because of another matter and insisted we talk tonight.

"Are you angry, Zoe? Frustrated, maybe? Elated?"

I nodded, twisted the wedding ring on my finger and looked at Rob Morton. "Any reason why I shouldn't feel elation? I took out that creep who shot Lopez and Ticer." Scum

13

like Garcia should not be allowed to roam the street, I thought.

"I understand your elation. That's normal. How about anger?"

You bet I'm angry, I thought. I'm angry that he shot Byron and got away with it. I'm angry because he's been free for eight months and Byron will never be free. But I knew that sounded cold and bent on revenge. That response would only get me in deep trouble, trouble I could do without.

I glanced around at Doc's bookcase filled with medical tomes and noticed for the first time, one shelf devoted to little toy cars. My brother, Chip, had once collected cars like these, I thought, *Hot Wheels*, I think they're called. Doc's cars were every color and shape but most looked like sports cars. Guess his slow-paced real life was filled with fast-paced dreams.

Instead of mentioning my anger, I asked, "Uh . . . how is Lopez, anyway? Is he going to make it?" My voice sounded funny, tinny, like it was coming from inside an old well.

"Lopez is fine. Remember? I told you he's out of surgery. He's going to be okay." Rob Morton's voice was quiet and firm, but it had that tinny sound also.

Morton wasn't a medical doctor, but had a degree in behavioral sciences, I think. We all called him "Doc" anyway. If I'd ever tried to conjure up a psychologist, he would look exactly like Doc: not too tall, a bit of a paunch, dark hair dusted with gray streaks framing his round, almost child-like face. He looked somewhere in his late forties and the reading glasses perched on his short upturned nose magnified his hazel-colored eyes.

"And Ticer?"

A small spiral notebook seemed to command his attention. "The doctors aren't sure yet, but she may lose partial use of her hand." He raised his eyes briefly to meet mine, then made a note on a page.

"Oh, yeah. You told me all this when I first came in. Why can't I remember?"

"That'll happen for a day or two. It's nothing to worry about. The brain's just off duty, trying to deal with the trauma." He reached for my hand and squeezed it briefly.

"Why didn't he give himself up, Doc?"

"Who knows Zoe?" Morton shrugged.

"He shot first, Doc. It was him or me."

"Garcia had already shot Lopez and Ticer. He tried to shoot you. You didn't do anything wrong."

"But why, why, why?"

"Maybe we'll know more when the investigation is over, Zoe," he said. "How's the nausea?"

My mouth felt as if some dental apparatus had sucked out all the saliva. And my eyes felt gritty. I rubbed them and tried to moisten my lips with my tongue. It didn't help.

Doc noticed my problem, got up and filled a paper cup with water and handed it to me.

I sipped, feeling only total exhaustion. "I . . . uh, don't know." I yawned. "Nothing seems . . . real, yet. I guess the fact this suspect turned out to be Garcia doesn't yet compute. Am I making sense?" I yawned again. "Excuse me."

"Yes. And I think now we'd better get you home. You need rest. You're at the bottom of your emotional well. And tomorrow at two you have an appointment to be questioned by Internal Affairs. You'll need to be alert then." He paused and the corners of his mouth turned up. "Don't be shocked when they try to make you feel like you did something wrong."

He stood and patted my arm. "All you have to do is tell them the truth. Don't let their techniques get under your skin. They might even try to make you angry."

"Why? I know they do it, but why?"

"Someone decided a few years ago that treating the officer as a suspect worked better. When a person gets defensive that person sometimes blurts out things, things the investigators hope comes closer to the truth." He offered his hand. I took it and stood. "Do you need anything to help you sleep?" he asked. "I can call one of the M.D.s for a prescription."

As I shook my head "no," my body did one of those involuntary shivers. When I was little, Mamma always said those shivers meant someone just walked over your grave. I never could understand how your grave got walked on when you weren't in it yet, but my mother's word was the law back then and I didn't question it or her. When the shudder ended, I felt as if I had shaken off the past few hours, letting them fall to the floor like dead leaves from a ficus tree.

"I don't like pills," I told Morton and my voice sounded more like my own. "But, boy *do* I want a drink." My mouth tasted like the back alley of a Sixth Street gin-joint. I managed a brief smile. "Something a little stronger than water."

"Alcohol probably isn't a good idea. Take a warm bubble bath and then, if you absolutely have to, drink *one* glass of wine." He walked out into the hall and held a murmured conversation with someone I couldn't see. When he came back, he said, "Officer Jacks will drive you home."

"I can drive," I stopped. "Oh, my car's not here. Okay. If someone can run me—"

"You live near the auditorium, don't you? You can pick up your car tomorrow."

"It's only a few blocks. I'll be fine, Doc. Quit hovering."

He smiled but his voice sounded firm. "I don't want you driving tonight. You could do damage to someone else if you have an accident, okay?"

When I nodded in agreement, he continued. "I'll see you

tomorrow before I.A. does. Try to rest; sleep is nature's best healer."

A uniform patrolman stood in the doorway. His eyes were dark, his nose long and his mouth puckered as if he'd just sucked on a sour lemon. "Did you call me, sir?"

"Jacks, this is Officer Barrow. Please drive her home and stay as long as she wants you."

"Yes, sir."

Officer Jacks's expression didn't change, and when I gave him directions to my apartment, he grunted. He did ask if we went right or left inside my apartment complex drive, then pulled into the parking space I indicated and killed the engine. I got out and he followed me to my front door.

To his credit, Jacks offered to stay with me but I'd felt strange vibes emanating from him. I don't know if he hated female cops in general or me in particular, but I didn't need the negativity that surrounded him. I insisted he return to duty. After I thanked him he stood at attention until I'd entered my front door and locked it. I watched him through a slit in the mini-blinds as he stiff-legged it back to his patrol car and drove off into the night.

My cats complained with loud meows when I came in and they rubbed against my legs. I stutter-stepped as they danced in front of me to the kitchen. As soon as their bowls had food and fresh water, I headed to the bathroom.

I took Doc's advice about the bubble bath and each time the water grew cool, I added more hot. My muscles relaxed and it felt great. A whole hour passed before I looked at my fingers, which looked pretty much like last week's shriveled apple cores, and crawled out.

The bath didn't relieve that bone-weariness, I thought, as I snuggled into a terry cloth robe. Doc's suggestion of a single glass of wine was probably a good one, but I poured a healthy shot of straight Kentucky bourbon instead. Maybe the whiskey would get rid of that awful taste, because two separate brushings hadn't touched it.

The message light on my answering machine caught my attention. I listened first to Lianne Crowder, my best friend since our academy days, and then next to my boss, Lieutenant Hamilton. Both asked me to call back no matter how late. I knew these friends had good intentions and were concerned about my state of mind, but what I needed was rest, not hand holding.

I couldn't not call back, however. Hamilton first, I decided, and when asked if I needed company he didn't press when I said no. "See you tomorrow," he said.

It wasn't that easy with Lianne. She took a belligerent tone. Insisted that I shouldn't be alone, but I finally convinced her to stay home. Shortly after hanging up the phone, I crawled into bed.

Maybe reality hadn't set in yet. Maybe I'd need their company tomorrow and tomorrow and tomorrow, but not tonight.

Just before I drifted off, the phone rang. I picked up the receiver next to the bed but no one was there. At least they didn't breathe or talk or do anything. I hung up and rolled over. "Wrong number. Some drunk," I mumbled. Although I do have an unlisted number, I still get random wrong numbers.

My dreams were full of bad guys chasing me and laughing when I fired my gun at them and then they disappeared into a puff of smoke.

At ten a.m. I awoke feeling as if I'd drunk a half-gallon of cheap wine. Ah, sweet memories of high school and college. A shower helped, but the toast I made and tried to eat didn't stay down. This gagging and heaving stuff could get old fast, I thought.

the back end opens into a dining alcove with bay windows. Childhood memories felt comforting when I'd decided to rent out the house I shared with Byron and moved into an apartment.

The windows let in light, although an overcast sky hid today's sunshine. It was a normal day for January in Austin, Texas, even if my day wasn't exactly normal.

While I poured coffee, Lianne drew up a chair to the round oak table that had once belonged to my grandmother and filled me in on how Garcia had robbed a convenience store and pistol-whipped the old man who worked there. The clerk had managed to pull himself up, call 911, and give a description of the suspect before he'd passed out.

She said, "Word went out that the suspect was spotted on foot near Palmer Auditorium. Lopez responded and got shot. Then Ticer showed up. She should have waited for backup."

"Her adrenaline got too high to think it through."

Lianne nodded and said, "Then you got involved."

I nodded.

She looked closely at me and asked, "Did you know it was Garcia? Wait, I don't want to know the answer to that."

Then I said, "No. I did *not* know it was Garcia; how could I?"

Lianne grinned and changed the subject. "Did you sleep at all? You look like the devil." Lianne has one of those complexions that's never had a pimple or a blackhead and she probably will never even wrinkle. Fatigue wouldn't dare show on her face.

"Gee, thanks," I said, knowing she wasn't being a smart-aleck even if she sounded like one. "I hate compliments this early in the morning."

She shrugged. "What else are friends for? A little blush on the cheeks would sparkle you up. Don't you have a cover stick for those dark circles?"

She shooed me to the bathroom and stood in the doorway while I applied faint color to my face.

"Much better," she said. "By the way, I checked with the hospital this morning. Lopez and Ticer are both happy to be alive. The convenience store clerk is critical but improving. Jesse Garcia is the only one who'll not be around to enjoy today."

"Lianne, women are supposed to be negotiators, not killers. I wish I hadn't shot the little creep."

"Two things, Zoe. You've got to remember two things. One, most likely Garcia was cranked up." Lianne's tone was calm and matter of fact.

"You're just saying that to make me feel better."

Lianne made a sound like "Sheesh," before she walked down the hall to the living room. I dropped the cover stick in my make-up bag, closed the cabinet drawer and followed.

She was on the sofa when I reached the room. "Think about it," she said. "Garcia beat up an old man, shot Lopez and Ticer. These are definitely not the actions of a normal person."

"Okay," I said, "what's the other thing I'm supposed to remember?" I waited in the doorway.

"The most important one, honey. Better him than you."

I was glad to hear her say those words, trite as they might sound. I needed her vote of confidence this morning.

"Don't let that creep get you down," she said. "Don't let him win. You did what you had to do and that's that."

The Austin police headquarters building has a solid-brick-wall front rising an imposing five floors and faces east alongside Interstate Highway Thirty-five, between Seventh and Eighth Streets. There are no windows except for the ones directly over the main doors, making it look like a fortress.

Maybe the architect had a thing about castles because he put apertures on two sides, which wound up looking somewhat like turrets in my book.

All the cops call the interior counter "the doughnut" because that's more or less what it looks like. A circular counter with a caged room in the middle for the "doughnut hole." The chief and other official offices are on the fifth floor. If hordes of terrorists ever try to take the chief hostage it won't be easy. It takes a key card for the elevators to go up to that level. The building housed the usual departments: communications, robbery, homicide, forgery and on the lower basement level in the back of the building is the City/County Jail, manned by the Travis County Sheriff's department.

I gave my name to the officer on duty and after a brief wait I was taken upstairs and ushered into a sparsely furnished conference room. The Internal Affairs officer in charge of my questioning introduced himself as Lieutenant Andrew Nichols. I'd seen him around but didn't know him. A stocky-built fatherly type, about fifty-five, he had gray fringes encircling a bald head and wore black-rimmed glasses. His friendly, polite manner undoubtedly had been designed to put people at ease as he smiled and invited me to sit across from him.

Two other officers were also present. One, a painfully thin man in his late thirties, had dark hair and penetrating dark eyes. His round face was incongruous with his physique and his narrow lips were pressed together so tightly they almost disappeared. His nametag read J. Links.

The third officer was tall, well built, with sun-bleached blond hair, perhaps no more than twenty-eight. He looked like a California surfer-type. Teenaged girls of my era would probably have called him "a hunk," but his narrowed blue eyes gave me the heebie-jeebies. His nametag read B. Proctor and we had graduated from the academy the same year. We were never what you'd call pals but we'd been comfortable around each other until he moved up to Internal Affairs.

Lieutenant Nichols asked if I'd read my statement aloud to be certain it was accurate. I took the papers that had been typed from my verbal account last night and cleared my throat. "At twenty-three hundred hours I was off-duty and returning home from a Lady Longhorns game. I was approximately two miles from Palmer when I heard dispatch say, 'Officer needs assistance. Shots fired.'"

The words faded and I saw it in my mind in great detail, like a video playing slow motion in my mind. Like I was at Palmer Auditorium once again.

The officer had groaned when I had squatted next to him. His olive skin deathly pale, his eyes closed and the radio microphone dangled in the air beside him. A dark puddle spread on the ground next to him. His uniform looked dark and wet near his left hip. I finally located the metallic nametag pinned to his navy shirt.

"Officer Lopez?" His eyes opened, tried to focus, but closed again. "Help's on the way." I could hear the sirens of the approaching squad cars. Every car in the sector would be here in seconds.

I remembered thinking, Ohmigod, he's going to die sitting right here. I wanted to lay him down or take him in my arms or something, but I knew better than to move him. "Please, please don't die on me," I told him.

"Ticer's in there—basement," Lopez coughed. "Alone. Help 'er."

A gunshot came from inside. I pulled my gun from its holster inside my police fanny pack. I tossed a mental coin. Wait for backup or go to the aid of an officer named Ticer? No contest. I crept down the stairs and entered the lower-level door, which

23

stood open. Two dim security lights gave out a poor light but my eyes adjusted fairly quick. At the bottom of the stairs, I heard first a whimpering sound, then what sounded like something being drug across the concrete floor.

That whimper gave me hope for Ticer and spurred me forward. I remembered the layout from attending a book and paper show earlier in the year. The hallway opened onto a small lobby-cum-registration room, which in turn led into the large exhibit room on the right. On the left were the men's and women's restrooms.

I gave a cautious peek around the first doorway. Clear. I slipped inside and moved as quick and as quiet as a cockroach walking on tiptoes to the second doorway of the larger room. I looked around the corner of the doorjamb. A back hallway at the far end of the room gave off a soft fluorescent glow but the remainder of the room only had a few dim security lights.

Tables and folding chairs, boxes and packing crates looked ominous in the semi-darkened room. Strange shapes rose up in the air and I realized the room had been partially set up for some type of show.

Suddenly my eyes were drawn to two dark shapes moving at a snail's pace about fifty feet to my left. The woman's right arm and hand dangled. The suspect had his right arm around her waist as he pushed and shoved her before him. Ticer whimpered and begged to be let loose. But she didn't struggle and that worried me.

I spotted what looked like a gun in the male's left hand and ducked behind a large wooden crate. "Police," I said. "Give it up now." I steadied my gun with both hands. They kept moving towards me slowly and I could see blood stringing from the woman's hand.

He threw Ticer to the floor and turned pointing his gun in my direction.

"Police," I said again. "Hold it right—" He fired at me

before I could finish.

I fired back. Bam, bam. Two shots. Just as I'd been taught.

It was over in less than three minutes. I had killed the suspect and immediately after that cops swarmed in and eventually someone found the switch and turned on the full lights.

A male officer asked, "Did you do that?" and he pointed to Garcia.

"Yes."

"You got him once in the shoulder and then dead center in the heart," he said. "It looks like a good shoot to me." He patted my arm reassuringly. Every officer who came in said and did all they could to give me confidence and to reassure me. And even though this man had used their fellow officers as targets their mood was somber. Taking the life of another human being was not something to feel elation about tonight.

Nausea had rolled in my stomach and I had to take several deep breaths to keep it from spewing out and embarrassing myself in front of everyone.

My hands began shaking as if I'd been transported into the midst of a blue norther. I clenched my fists and hooked my thumbs into my Levi pockets so no one would see.

"Officer Barrow?" Nichols's voice brought me back to the I.A. debriefing room, but I had not heard his question.

"Sorry, sir. Didn't hear you." I realized my hands were jammed tight in my pockets.

No one would ever see signs of weakness coming from me. Even in today's enlightened world some male cops still think women aren't tough enough to handle police work. I knew it was only the adrenaline last night that caused my hands to shake, and today? Reliving that moment had seemed real.

"I asked if your statement is true to the best of your knowledge?" Nichols asked.

"Yes, sir."

"And you're sure you identified yourself to that suspect as being a police officer?"

"Yes, sir. At least twice, maybe even three times."

The questions went along in that vein for a few minutes, then began to change. Nichols's voice took on a harsher tone and he didn't look like the fatherly type anymore.

And Officer Links got into the act, both men throwing questions out, rapid-fire, in random sequence.

"Officer Barrow, why did you go to Palmer Auditorium in the first place?"

"Did you see Lopez get shot?"

"Why didn't you wait for back-up?"

"Weren't you off duty?"

"How many shots did Garcia fire at you?"

"What time did you turn on your walkie-talkie?"

"What reason did you have for going to Palmer?" This last came from Links.

Had they not heard anything I'd said? This was total bull and they knew it. "*Any* cop will respond to an officer-assist call. You know that."

"So," asked Nichols, "are you telling us you didn't know Jesse Garcia was the suspect?"

"No, sir."

"Didn't you hear Patrolman Lopez say the suspect matched a description of Jesse Garcia?"

"No. Garcia supposedly was in Mexico," I said. "I never heard Lopez's voice over the radio. I only heard dispatch and responded. Surely this can be verified by the 911 tapes."

Officer Links came at me again. "But you did identify the suspect as your husb—Officer Barrow's shooter, didn't you?"

"Someone else ID'd him afterwards, not me. I had no idea who the suspect was until several minutes after the shooting."

Officer Proctor sat through this whole exchange with his

arms folded, not asking questions nor even speaking. Now, he tilted his head to one side, but he didn't look like an inquisitive puppy. He reminded me of a prosecutor I'd seen in a movie once. "Officer Barrow, you have been involved in two shooting incidents, is that right?"

"Two? Not really."

"Officer, you shot a suspect in the leg a couple of years ago and this is your second shooting incident, is it not?"

I looked at him steadily. His face had a look that shouted—gotcha.

"In that earlier shooting," I said, "it was never determined whether my bullet or my partner's hit the suspect."

His voice softened a bit. "But that was the first incident and this is the second, is that not correct?"

Technically he was right and he obviously wanted me to admit it.

"That is correct."

"And on that first occasion you did shoot the suspect in the leg? Is that correct?"

"The bullet went all the way through the man's leg and was never found. Neither my partner nor I ever knew which one of us hit him. Both of us fired at the suspect at the same time."

"Kinda trigger happy, aren't you?" Nichols's tone was patronizing.

"I've been with APD for almost nine years and have only fired my weapon twice. No. I would not say I was trigger happy."

Proctor changed the subject abruptly. "Isn't it a fact that you've been roaming the streets at night searching for Jesse Garcia?"

I'd never admit anything—old classmate or not. "No, I've never spent time searching for Garcia."

The thin officer, J. Links, decided it was time to put in his two cents' worth again. "Is there any way Garcia could have known who you were? Could he have known you're the wife of the policeman he shot last year?"

"No. I doubt he ever knew Byron's wife was a police officer. And I didn't introduce myself last night."

"Garcia comes from a big family," said Nichols. "Someone from his family would know who you are from the newspaper and TV."

I shrugged. "Are you saying he deliberately set this up to lure me some way? How would he know I'd respond to that assist call? I'm sorry sir, this line of questioning doesn't make sense."

These guys were getting ridiculous and I was tired of the whole thing. They had made it clear in the beginning this was only an inquiry and I was free to go at any time. I chose now. I stood. "If there is nothing else?"

The silence in the room stretched as the three officers looked at each other, some unseen message going between them. Andrew Nichols cleared his throat and spoke. "Okay, Officer Barrow. You're dismissed for now, but don't forget you're subject to recall at any time, so don't—"

"Leave town?" It sounded absurd even as I said it.

Nichols sighed. "I was going to warn you not to discuss this interview with anyone. Do not make this a topic of department gossip."

I ignored his remark and asked. "May I go back on duty?"

"Administrative duty. Not on the street."

"I've got cases working."

"Your supervisor's already reassigned your case load."

"For how long?"

"Depends. On what we find out. You know the routine."

Yes, I knew the routine.

The nursing home where Byron Barrow lay, breathing on

his own but totally unaware of anything, was clean and cheerful. The two-story, native-limestone building in far North Austin is old, built around the same time as the state mental hospital. Only five blocks east of the interstate, then you turn and head north for a couple of miles on one of those country roads that Austin has in abundance. The place stood barely inside the city limits with pastureland on two sides and trees surrounding a small lake behind it. It took only minutes to drive from either my job or my apartment.

I parked in the visitor's lot and my stomach got that usual knot of ice. I must have been about ten when my mother took me to see her mother at the Austin State Hospital. My grandmother's drinking had become a problem and she'd been admitted to dry out. This was not the same place but this gray limestone building brought back unpleasant memories of too many family arguments.

The flower print sofas and chairs looked pretty and are practical being made of a heavy-duty plastic to resist soil. Numerous live plants add a warm tone to the stark white walls, as do the pastoral scenic pictures.

"Hi, Naomi," I greeted the nurse on duty. "How are you today?"

"Hey, Zoe. Okay and you?"

"Hanging in there." I was anxious to see my husband so I didn't stay to chat as I sometimes did. "Is my fella ready for company?"

"You bet. He's been waiting for you."

I walked down the hall, speaking briefly to a couple of patients along the way. Ninety-five percent of the residents here are people over seventy, many stroke and Alzheimer's victims. It's a clean trying-to-be-cheerful warehouse of the living.

A quick glance inside Byron's room reminded me I needed

to change the posters and cards on the wall. The ones there were getting a faded look and I tried to keep things bright and cheery, not only for his sake but for mine, too.

There was no change in Byron but that wasn't surprising, he always looked the same—the perfect picture of health as long as his right arm and leg were covered. His right side was the one paralyzed. He's lost some weight and muscle tone. Physical therapists exercised his limbs regularly.

His black hair is kept in a crew cut by the nursing home barber, it's easier to care for that way. His blue-green eyes are often open, but there's nothing there. No light, no life, only the vacant stare of no one at home.

"Hi, Sweetie," I said, pulling the bedside chair up next to the bed rail and taking his good hand in mine. "How's it going today?"

One-sided conversations are difficult, but no one knew how much he might be able to hear. I'd told him from the beginning who was suspected of shooting him and kept him informed of the progress or the lack thereof on catching Garcia.

"I've had a rough time the last two days," I began, detailing the shooting and the I.A. sessions. "Since the suspect was Jesse Garcia, it's been the weirdest experience."

Byron made no sign he heard.

"Honey, I was so surprised when this guy was identified as Garcia. And it's scary because they've implied I *knew* it was Garcia all along. That I was on some sort of vendetta to kill this guy who shot you."

Again there was no response. I couldn't believe it. For the past twenty-four hours I'd held on to the hope that Byron would understand what had happened—that when he heard, it would bring him out of this comatose state.

"Honey, don't you see? It's over. You can wake up now." I

took his face in my hands and looked directly into his vacant eyes.

Cynthia, one of the evening shift aides, chose that moment to stick her head inside. "Ms. Barrow, it's time for dinner. Do you want a few more minutes?"

I nodded, not quite trusting my voice and mercifully she left. I never stayed for his meals. It was too painful to watch my dignified husband being spoon-fed like a baby.

"Oh, Byron. I need you so much right now because I'm really scared." He lay there in his own little world not connecting with mine in any way.

"The doctors are right, darling. You'll never come back, will you?"

On December 27, 1839 the village of Waterloo was officially incorporated and became the city of Austin. Not everyone was happy about the new capital city: Sam Houston was quoted as saying Austin was "the most unfortunate site upon earth." (Compiled from: *Austin American Statesman Monthly Almanac* and Austin History Center Records.)

Chapter 3

Austin, Texas was named for Stephen F. Austin, known as the father of Texas because he brought in the first colonists. It's one of the state's most unusual geographic areas—a meeting point of the Edwards Plateau, the Coastal Plains and the Blackland Prairie, with the Balcones Fault cutting through the center of Travis County. Geology was never my strong suit, but this stuck in my mind because of the added potential for disaster, despite assurances that all is stable now.

There's even an extinct volcano, known in recent years as Pilot's Knob, lying in the southern part of the county. I fully expect it to erupt one day, even though the experts say it's impossible. Fortunately, the city thoughtfully built a huge water storage tank on the summit and millions of gallons of water should put out the fires and stop the lava flow immediately should I happen to be correct. Austin's other unique topography is how it was built along the meandering banks of the lower Colorado River.

Austin was once known as Waterloo-on-the-Colorado although "why" escapes me. One of the state's founding fathers, Mirabeau Bonaparte Lamar, who later became the President of the Republic of Texas, probably had something to do with that name. Mirabeau's middle name came from an uncle who had admired Napoleon. If Miss Durrett, my fifth-grade history teacher, ever explained the connection to Waterloo in any detail, I probably slept right through her class. Even though the pretty redhead was my idol, history was too boring to keep me awake.

I do remember Miss Durrett explaining how Lamar envisioned a city to be built on this scenic location, the seat of government for the state, and how he wanted to honor Stephen Austin and Stephen's father, Moses, by calling the city Austin. He would probably spin in his grave to see how traffic chokes and clogs his scenic city today. And I can almost hear General Houston saying, "See I told you this was a lousy choice."

The portion of the city that includes the capitol building, the governor's mansion and the major portion of downtown, sits on the north shore of Town Lake. This lake was formed by the damming of the lower Colorado River and it's only one in a chain of dams and lakes stretching along for miles known as the Highland Lakes: Inks Lake, Lake Buchanan, Lake L.B.J., Lake Travis, Lake Austin, and Lake Marble Falls. The Lower Colorado River Authority probably never dreamed of the tourist potential caused by their actions, but Austin is known as the pretty part of this vast state. It's one major reason I live here. Great Mexican food is another.

The complex where I live sits on the south shore of Town Lake and my apartment with its glass door and deck faced both the water and downtown. The lake with trees and a hike and bike trail alongside usually eased my daily frustrations just by looking at it, and to live close to the pulse of my city made life interesting.

My pager beeped as I angled my car into my assigned space at my complex.

Danged old electronic leash. I read the number recorded there—555-2800. It was unfamiliar. "Probably a snitch," I said aloud.

Sometimes they call from strange places, especially when the weekend rolled around. The speed with which an informant found information to trade on Friday was uncanny.

The steady rain which had fallen all day and the mind-chilling fact that I had not heard anything from Internal Affairs put me in a most uncivil mood. I preferred to enter my den, remove both clothing and shoes and make a renewed acquaintance with a Coors Light. Later . . . maybe . . . I'd see what 555-2800 wanted.

Melody and Lyric gave me a purring welcome home and, while they nibbled at their fresh food, I pulled a beer out of the fridge. I popped it open, drank a big swallow and threw a longing look out the glass doors to the deck, but it was too wet and yucky out today.

I stripped; scratching where my bra etched lines on my skin, pulled on a pair of sweats and plopped on the sofa with my bare feet on the coffee table. The first beer was gone and I'd already begun a second before I searched through my address book and found no listing for 555-2800.

"Curiosity, they say, is what killed the cat," I told the napping Lyric, who'd curled into my lap and nudged at my hand for petting until he slept. He opened one eye briefly before curling his body tighter, and ignored me. I sighed and picked up the phone. Before calling anyone I didn't know, someone who had paged me, I always punched in a blocker code so they wouldn't get my unlisted phone number on a caller ID.

"Avery Peppard." The male voice said in a deep rich baritone.

I didn't recognize the voice or the name. "This is Zoe Barrow."

"Thank you for returning my call."

Who's Avery Peppard? I wondered. And how had he gotten my pager number?

"I got your number from Levi Barrow," he said as if I'd spoken the question aloud.

Levi Barrow was Byron's father—my father-in-law. "Yes, Mr. Peppard?"

"Uh, Levi said, uh, said you'd be able to help me. I need to talk to a police officer." He cleared his throat. "Are you free for dinner?"

I couldn't keep the irritation from my voice. "Afraid I don't fix traffic tickets."

"I wouldn't expect you to. It's a little more serious than a ticket." He cleared his throat again. "Look, I know this is short notice, but I must talk to you. If tonight isn't convenient, how about breakfast tomorrow morning?"

I wasn't exactly thrilled about going out again tonight, what with the lousy weather and my even lousier mood, but if Levi Barrow told the man to call, I couldn't in good conscience refuse. My father-in-law was too good a friend to ignore his wishes.

Besides, curious cats usually find ways to satisfy their curiosity even when it turns out to be dangerous. "Dinner tonight would be best," I told Peppard. "I don't do mornings well."

From Austin's earliest days—fairs, theater, music, shops, balls, cotillions—many specializing in food and drink, were the major social activities for the town folks. It's true even today.

Several years ago a decision was made to tart-up a portion of downtown and an entertainment district was created along and around Sixth Street (originally Pecan Street) where clubs, taverns, restaurants and boutiques flourish to cater to The University (as the university of Texas is known) faculty and students, the myriad of government workers, the tourists and, of course, the locals. Cooper's Corner is one such restaurant, a remodeled house on the fringes of the near west side of downtown. The area is one of my favorite places.

I took a quick look at Treaty Oak as I parked nearby. This is the infamous old oak that had been poisoned with an herbicide a few years ago. A foul deed which had upset many Texans. People across the country were aghast when the man was sent to prison, but it sent a clear message—don't mess with Texas landmarks. The tree still lives but will never recover. Byron still lives, but may never recover either. That was something I didn't like to think about.

It was five minutes before the hour when I arrived. The decor inside was pink and turquoise with highly polished hardwood floors gleaming under my feet. It reminded me of a yuppie-fied Chili's restaurant.

A small sign informed: Wait To Be Seated, except at the moment no one was present to seat me. I remembered coming here for lunch two or three years ago but wasn't sure I'd been in since so I spent time looking around. I revised my earlier assessment; it was a step up from Chili's—nicer, or maybe classier was the better word. The dining area looked full, everyone in a typical TGIF mood and having a good time. A waiter bustled by and tantalizing aromas from the tray of food he carried made my mouth water.

When the hostess came to inquire if I was dining alone tonight, I said I was joining Mr. Peppard. She smiled and told me he was waiting. I followed her to a table where a tall man, probably in his early fifties, stood as he saw us approach. He was dressed in a charcoal-colored suit that fit him as only a tailor-made can. His tie, a light gray silk with a floral pattern of mauve, ivory and charcoal, picked up a nearly invisible mauve thread in his suit. He wore a crisp white shirt and gold links peeked from his cuffs. His medium brown hair held a few gray temple strands, looking like they were painted on. A pair of blue-gray eyes looked at me, and I noticed his square jaw jutted almost as much as Jay Leno's but it somehow added to his attractiveness.

I'd fretted about what to wear because dressing fancy never excites me, and so I'd decided on an ensemble consisting of a pair of black slacks with a turquoise knit shell. A black blazer and a pair of black suede pumps with one-inch heels, topped things off and I'd even grabbed a pair of tiny loop silver earrings and a silver chain to add. Semi-casual is haute couture for Austin's laid-back atmosphere but I'd had a feeling Mr. Peppard would be dressed in a more business-like attire and I'd chosen right.

Peppard held out his hand and a faint smile touched his full lips. "Mrs. Barrow?" He gave my hand a firm, yet brief, squeeze. "I'm Avery Peppard. Please sit down."

"And please call me Zoe—it rhymes with Joe."

His lips twitched. "Okay, Zoe it rhymes with Joe, I'm Avery."

"Nice place," I said. "I've sort of forgotten about it."

He glanced around, almost as if seeing the place for the first time. "This *is* a great place," he said. "I'm here about once a week." His glance also alerted the waiter, who came and hovered.

"Would you like wine?" Avery asked. "Or something else?"

"A glass of wine would be excellent. You choose."

"Fall Creek Chardonnay, 1997," Peppard said to the waiter, but looked at me for approval. When I didn't comment, he said, "It's an excellent white."

"I'm sure it'll be fine," I said. "I don't know much about wine, I just usually order the house white." I noticed Avery staring at me.

"When Levi said Byron's wife was a police officer, Zoe, I don't know what I expected," he said. "But it's a pleasant surprise to find you're so pretty, so feminine."

"You don't think attractive women ever become police officers?"

He looked a bit startled. "Well, no . . . well, maybe. I guess my mental image of women police officers is stereotyped."

"Big, tough, butch?"

"Maybe. Something like that." Peppard scratched his left earlobe. "A girl as pretty as you could be almost anything. Why a cop?"

"Probably because I liked the uniform."

"What?"

"I always wanted to look really cool."

Avery Peppard managed a brief smile. "You're putting me on and I deserved it."

"Only a little. But to answer your question, I wanted to be a cop in order to help people. But to be totally honest, at first it was because I fell in love with Byron. What he liked I liked. Whatever he did, I wanted to do.

"But to take all the romance out of it, my favorite uncle was a cop killed in the line of duty up in Fort Worth when I was fourteen. His funeral was so impressive I made a promise I'd take his place one day."

I did not add that when I met Byron I was hell-bent on self-destruction. My parents loved me but my mother has a tendency to smother and I rebelled.

This went on for about two years and one evening Byron hauled me and a few of my pals downtown for drinking beer and disturbing the peace. We weren't driving, we were hanging out at a convenience store parking lot and mouthing off at the customers.

All our parents had been called, except no one answered at my house. Byron drove me home, waited for my folks and for several months after that he kept an eye on me, calling occasionally to ask how I was. It wasn't until after I straightened

guess I'm reluctant to begin."

I sipped the wine. It *was* good. I told him so then asked, "How do you know Levi?"

"Oh. Levi and I have known each other forever." And he detailed their school days together up through college and how he'd married Jean Barrow's younger sister, Susan, and how they'd moved to California. "I was a young, hard drinking, unemployed jerk. The Barrows would have nothing to do with us."

Peppard went on to explain how after age forty he'd settled down and become a success, but by then Susan received too much pleasure from playing a martyr and the split was inevitable, although it took another fifteen years to happen.

That explained a lot. I knew that until recently my mother-in-law and her sister had been estranged, but Jean Barrow never hinted at what caused the estrangement. A couple of years ago a vague story went around the family about how Aunt Susan's husband had left her for a younger woman and immediately Susan had been welcomed back into the family circle.

"We were only divorced two weeks when I remarried and moved back to Austin."

"That raised a few eyebrows, I'll bet."

"And a few noses, too. Maybe I hit the middle age crazies, but I fell in love. Probably for the first time in my life. And I paid dearly for it. My old friends snubbed me and that hurt."

"But you did contact Levi, today," I said.

"Yes, because I didn't know who . . . I would have preferred going to Byron, but since he's . . . uh—"

"In a coma?"

He nodded. "Didn't *like* going to Levi, but I had no choice. I needed someone I could trust. Someone who'd tell me the best way to handle this, uh, problem and I knew Byron's wife was with the police." Avery was drinking his wine like it was water. "I couldn't even tell Levi all the details, just enough for him to give me your home and your pager numbers."

Peppard finished his first glass of wine and poured another. He asked if I wanted more, but I'd barely begun on mine. "It's excellent wine," I said, "but I'm a sipper."

He smiled and, for the first time the smile extended all the way to his eyes. "Guess my nerves are showing, but telling you some of my background has helped. Let's order dinner and afterwards I'll tell you why I wanted to meet you."

"Good idea. What do you recommend?"

The waiter materialized and hovered again while Peppard recommended several dishes. I chose the mesquite-grilled chicken breast with bean sprouts and baby squash.

We talked small talk, the usual stuff, and he told me about his software company. I had the impression he was successful. Something about a start-up company and then going public with the stock. Of course, with the recent market downturn, maybe things weren't too good right now.

When we finished eating and the waiter had brought over coffee, Peppard cleared his throat. He still looked a bit uncomfortable, but jumped right in. "My wife, Mary Margaret, is having an affair."

"Perhaps you need a lawyer, not a police officer," I said, in a neutral tone to keep from sounding flippant.

"I, uh, have good reason to believe she and her . . . uh, boyfriend are planning to have me killed."

That could make it a police matter. "Why do you think . . . I mean, do you have any proof?"

"Not . . . I overheard . . . on the telephone when they suddenly discussed hiring a . . . a hit man."

"Your wife's boyfriend? Is he a business associate of

yours? An acquaintance? One of your friends?"

"He's no one I know. I'm quite certain of that."

"I guess I still don't understand," I said. "Why come to me?"

"Because from some things the man said, I mean from the way he used words—his attitude, his lingo. I don't know, but I think my wife's lover is a cop."

Austin's first experiment using the newfangled telephone took place on December 9, 1877 and along with conversation and several corny jokes, a minister's daughter sang an old hymn, *Almost Persuaded*. The song was heard six miles away on wires stretched between the telegraph office and Dr. Clark's store. Austin's first telephone exchange opened in 1881 with seventeen business subscribers. (Compiled from: *Austin American Statesman Monthly Almanac* and Austin History Center Records.)

Chapter 4

"How can I tell the police that one of their fellow officers wants to have me killed?"

"You *are* between that proverbial rock and a hard place. And it's not exactly something you can ask your wife about, is it?"

"No. I feel helpless and I can't stand feeling like that. I guess I'm a take-charge sort of guy. What scares me most is that a cop knows a hundred ways to make a murder look like an accident."

"You're right but I honestly don't know what I can do."

"What? Why not? You're a cop. Can't you record her phone calls?"

"Sure, but listen a minute," I said. "Wire-tapping is not legal without a court order and there's nothing I could say here to convince a federal judge . . ."

The look on his face was still disbelieving. "Can't you arrest him?"

"Avery. You don't even know this man's name, do you?" Peppard shook his head. "Say we issued a John Doe warrant—where do we go to serve it?"

His face brightened slightly. "Oh, wait. Once she called him Cowboy or something like that."

I shook my head. "We can't just grab someone out of thin air. And why do you think this man is a cop?"

"You have to understand that what I overheard was by accident."

I nodded.

Eavesdropping. It happened as easily as in the late 1880s

when you could listen in on everyone's party line.

"I had just returned from a business trip, dropped off my briefcase in the study, when the telephone rang. I automatically picked up, but my wife said 'hello' before I could speak."

"Then a man on the other end said, 'Hello, Babe.' "

Avery had not recognized the voice and thought the man had a wrong number. "Then M.M. told this guy she couldn't talk long because Avery was due any minute. Suddenly I noticed her lovey-dovey tone, too.

"I was so shocked, I couldn't say anything. I couldn't believe it." The anguish in Peppard's face was evident. "I remember thinking this must be a nightmare."

"The man then mentioned something about putting the word out on the street to find this dude paroled from Huntsville who could take care of their problem. His words sounded like TV cop lingo," Avery said. "And fifteen thousand dollars was mentioned as a payment.

"Then she asked if there were any other way. And the guy said not if you want out rich."

"Maybe your wife . . . what did you say her name was?"

"Mary Anna Margaret, but everyone calls her M.M. With three names you have to shorten it."

"Maybe she's being coerced."

"Well, she did acquiesce to him. My wife is an independent, self-reliant young woman but not to this guy."

"Could she be on drugs?"

"Not to my knowledge. Yet it's quite obvious now that my wife does a lot of things without my knowledge."

"Have you had trouble in your marriage?"

He hesitated. "I won't deny we've had some problems. My god, M.M. is nearly twenty-five years younger. I've often felt she was restless—bored maybe—nothing serious. We'd discussed having a child several times. I think I'm too old to start a family and I've been quite adamant. Maybe that was a mistake."

He rubbed his earlobe and continued. "I'm trying to be honest here and yet I know I'm looking at things in hindsight. But the money angle boggles my mind."

"The fifteen thousand for a hit?"

"Not that. This guy told her how he knew she deserved more than the stinking few thousand she'd get in a divorce."

"A pre-nuptial agreement?"

Avery nodded. "Five hundred thousand."

"And what does she get if you die?"

"I have my company, property—"

"What's the bottom line?"

"Something in the neighborhood of fifteen million, but—"

I whistled softly. "That's a nice neighborhood."

". . . it's mostly on paper. I mean the half-million from the pre-nup would be close to the top mark on the cash that could be raised even if I up and died tomorrow."

"She *could* liquidate?"

"Not easily. The company is a corporation. There are shareholders. And with today's volatile market, not smart."

Plus he probably had at least a million dollars in life insurance. Sounds like a huge temptation in my book, but I didn't elaborate. I could almost see wheels turning in his head as if he were only now realizing all the implications.

"It's just that M.M. *never* acted like money was all that important," he said. "I mean, she enjoys what we have and what we can do, but she loves me—not my money."

He was aging visibly before my eyes and I thought it sad. The waiter asked if we needed anything and Peppard ordered more coffee. In a moment he said, "Zoe, can you help? If this guy is a cop, it's going to take a cop to catch him."

"With nothing more to go on . . ." I let the sentence trail. The only clues I could see were the mention of Huntsville and this guy's knowledge of a prisoner being released. I sipped my coffee. "Avery, I have one suggestion—hire a private eye."

He looked skeptical and I continued, "Look, a P.I. can follow Mrs. Peppard until she meets this guy, then the P.I. can follow him and find out who he is."

"Then you can arrest him."

"Avery. The last time I looked, it was not against the law to sleep with another man's wife."

He turned pale.

I probably shocked him by being blunt, but I wanted him to understand what I was saying. "Look I can't arrest the man even if you find out who he is. He would have to do some bodily harm to you."

"Okay, but he threatened to kill me."

"Not technically. You overheard a phone conversation between your wife and a man. That's entirely different." The thing I wasn't saying to him about his wife's involvement had not occurred to him yet.

"And it would be my word against his?"

"Yes. And even your word against your wife's. I don't think Mrs. Peppard will admit—"

The light suddenly dawned. "Oh no. M.M. could be arrested too, couldn't she?"

I was glad not to have to spell it out. "Yes, that's possible. But at this point, there's no proof of conspiracy, no proof even of the telephone call you say you overheard."

Avery's voice was sharp. "You think I made this all up?"

A police officer hears so many lies, sooner or later you learn to separate wheat from chaff, but he was a businessman and didn't get where he was without stretching the truth when necessary. I looked at him closely, "Uh, no. I don't think so."

"Ohhh man. You had to think it over."

"Avery, I just met you." I looked at my watch. "Until a little over an hour ago, I'd never laid eyes on you."

He was silent a moment thinking about what I said. "Okay. I can live with that. But what you're saying is that you won't help."

"Well, there's really nothing that I or the police *can* do right now. I suggest you vary your schedule and don't give out any information about your appointments to your wife—or to anyone else for that matter. Try not to let her know you suspect anything. You might consider hiring a bodyguard, but I still think your best bet is to hire a private investigator."

"Do you know someone?"

"I can ask around."

"I guess you're right," he said and looked me straight in the eyes. "One thing I worried about all last night and all day today was how could I ever get the police to believe me. Cops cover up for each other, don't they?"

"Contrary to some opinions, the officers I know and work with in my immediate department wouldn't cover up a murderer even if it was a fellow officer. However, this guy could be a deputy or a constable or even a private security cop.

"But," I said, "although I hate to think someone in our department is capable of something like this—it is possible. Crooked cops do exist in this world as we've discovered in the past few years."

A short time later, when Peppard and I left the restaurant I knew he definitely wasn't a happy camper.

My drive home was filled with thoughts how greed is often a stronger emotion than love. Avery Peppard was looking for a miracle, but I was fresh out of those. I honestly felt sorry for him. It would be horrible to discover the person you loved not only was playing around, but actually wanted you dead and was plotting to have it done.

What if Mrs. Peppard and her lover succeeded in killing Avery? How would I feel knowing that I had knowledge beforehand and not been able to prevent it?

"What a depressing thought," I said to the cats when I arrived home.

"Meow," said Lyric. We quickly established he had no answers either.

The next day I got the name of a private investigator for Peppard. A guy by the name of Warren Adams. I'd never met him but he'd been highly recommended to our office. Peppard said he'd call the man and I moved Peppard onto the back burner of my consciousness. My own problems were more pressing right now.

I harbored self-doubts about shooting Garcia. Sleeping and eating were among my most difficult problems. It felt like a stone the size of a fist had taken up residence in my stomach. If I got tired enough I could sleep, but often woke up from nightmares of shooting a policeman or Garcia and then couldn't get back to sleep. The Internal Affairs sessions left me drained. I reached a point where I could have shouted, "Yes, I'm glad. I'm glad I killed the bastard who ruined my life." But I never did.

The news media rehashed about Byron being shot and my shooting Garcia, but the public information officer shielded me totally. They knew my talking to them was off limits. Finally, an older couple in west Austin was brutally murdered in their home and I became *old* news.

Boredom became a constant companion. Just when I thought I would go totally bonkers from being on desk duty an urgent message from one of my confidential informants, Tami Louise Smuts came in on my voice mail. She wanted to see me as soon as I had some time. Tami's real surname is Smith but when I met her two years ago, she explained, "Who'd want to do business with a hooker named Smith?" I was surprised anyone would care about last names.

My idea was to go to my office and discuss the meet with my supervisor, Lieutenant Hamilton, but the place was deserted except for Kyle Raines.

Kyle's a big guy. Six feet and hits the scales at about two hundred. With his bushy auburn beard and dark brown eyes, he reminds me of a teddy bear. He doesn't look like a cop and is able to parlay that asset in undercover roles with great ease.

"Where is everyone?" I asked him.

He explained: some of the day shift had joined a drug task force and had busted a crack house around dawn. One person was off sick and the Loot was off doing something in Waco and wasn't expected back until afternoon.

I liked Kyle, but he was a major skirt chaser and being married had never slowed his activities. I'm not a prude, yet I had trouble dealing with it on a personal level. Mostly I felt people could do their own thing as long as it didn't hurt me, but I somehow found his behavior distasteful. Mostly I felt sorry for Kyle's wife.

I think he reminded me too much of my younger brother, Chip—charming, good-looking—and Chip had been a skirt-chaser until he fell in love and married Pat. Maybe that was Kyle's problem—he didn't truly love his wife.

And until I'd enlightened him, he sometimes let his piggy side rule his mouth. When Elizabeth Watson had been named chief of police and Sergeant Shauna Dreslinski became the first woman ever assigned to APD's homicide unit, I couldn't keep quiet and jumped down his throat.

We patched things up later and he never put women down

again in my presence. I did respect his work, as he was an excellent cop.

I sat at my desk to write out a memo for Lieutenant Hamilton about my meeting. I wanted something on record if anything came up later, since I couldn't officially walk the mean streets yet. My coffee cooled to lukewarm as I shoved things aside to make a clear spot. I get teased unmercifully about my desk—because it's always the messiest one. Like there is some XX (female) chromosome gene in me that demands that I have a neat desk. The phone rang and Kyle answered and began clandestine conversation, another woman, I assumed.

"Kyle, listen up," I said as I finished the memo. "I've got to travel."

He placed his hand over the mouthpiece.

"Meeting that person?"

Kyle knew Tami's name but acted like he didn't as she was my C.I. "At two," I said. "Depending on what she says today, we might have enough to get a warrant on that bozo out in the projects."

For the past few weeks Tami Louise had been feeding me information on a big dealer out at one of the projects and her information was fairly reliable. The dealer, one we'd targeted about six months ago, was someone we needed to get off the streets.

Kyle talked a few seconds longer, then hung up and grinned sheepishly. His cavalier attitude pushed my button and as usual I couldn't keep my mouth shut. "Kyle, why do you do that to your wife? She deserves better."

"I know. I hate myself but what do you want me to do?"

"Go home and take care of your lady."

"Just because you've given up sex, doesn't mean the rest of us should." His voice rose a little as he began to get defensive.

"I haven't given up—" I stopped when I heard the anger in my own voice. I bit the inside of my lip to keep from blurting more harsh words. He would do whatever he wanted to, no matter what I said.

"Sorry," Kyle said, "I don't mean anything. Uh, I mean with Byron lying up there." Kyle stared intently at a speck of something on his tie. "Oh crap . . ."

"Let's just drop it, okay? I'm sorry I opened my big mouth too. What you do is your business."

"Okay." He gave me one of his famous smiles. "Oh yeah, you got a phone call a few minutes ago when you were in the john." He picked up a pink telephone message pad and handed it to me. "Some guy named Peppard?"

"Thanks." I glanced at the note. Wondering what was up with Peppard, I called him back.

Private investigator Warren Adams had not had enough time to help Avery Peppard and did I know anyone else? I promised to find someone and get back to him.

Kyle said he'd met a new P.I. recently named Jason Foxx; an ex-cop from the Houston area who now lived here. "Your pal Lianne knows his aunt or something," Kyle said.

"Sounds good. Thanks Kyle." I called Peppard back and since he was out, left the information on his voice mail.

"When the boss comes in, Kyle, tell him I've put this memo in his IN box."

"Right. See you later, Zoe." There was no animosity in his voice or his smile.

I smiled back, glad we had nipped our little disagreement in the bud. Our working relationship was too important to the unit for arguments regarding our private lives. Besides, if he wanted to destroy his marriage, it wasn't my place to butt into things. Kyle had a lovely wife he'd never be faithful to and I had a comatose husband I couldn't play around on—it somehow seemed ironic, I thought, as I took the elevator to the garage level.

Tami was already at Denny's on Oltorf in South Austin when I arrived, sitting in a booth in the back and sipping from a mug of coffee. She was not exactly a pretty girl. Her thin face was all angles and her blonde hair had been bleached so often it had an orangey-red stiffness. Her big blue eyes had a hardness beyond her twenty-one years. But her personality was bubbly, giving her a cuteness that some men found attractive. And, if you added in the lushness of her young body, it was easy to see how she made a fairly successful living turning tricks.

Tami had worked as my snitch for nearly two years. I liked her.

I slid into the booth and waited until the waitress brought my coffee before I spoke. "What's happening? What's so urgent?"

She looked at me as if she'd never seen me before. "Did you really blow that Garcia guy away?" A note of awe tinged her East Texas twang.

I frowned and she lowered her voice.

"I read all about it in the papers," she said. "You're just like that cop that was on TV. You know, I forget her name. Blue Lady or something. They called her Dirty Harriet. She'd just pull out that big ol' three fifty-seven and blow away those bad guys."

"Look, Tami, I can't discuss . . ." It was crazy, but I felt my relationship with Tami suddenly shift and it was a change that made me uncomfortable. Elevating me to a heroine status because I'd killed a bad guy was not a role I relished. "It wasn't like anything you see on—"

"Man, it was so cool. Think I'm gonna get me a gun, learn how to shoot. Next time some little fart starts giving me a hard time, I'll blow his balls off."

Right, I thought, that's all we needed: hookers running around with loaded guns. "Wait a minute. If you pull a gun on someone, he might take it away from you and use it on you," I said. "Or what if you do shoot the sucker? You'll wind up going to jail for murder."

"Not if it's self-defense."

"But you'd have to prove you were in danger. Just because some guy starts giving you a hard time doesn't mean you can pull out a gun and start shooting."

Tami's mouth turned pouty; her lower lip pooched out and her mood went from excited to defensive. "I thought you were my friend. You just want to see me out there on the streets at the mercy of the sickos and the weirdos?"

"Tami, I don't want you on the street at all. I'd much rather see you get straight. Maybe go to school. Make something out of your life while you're young enough to do it."

"Yeah, well, let me clue you in, Miss Straight and Narrow. It's too late for me. Who's gonna pay for school? Who's gonna hand me a job paying what I make now laying on my back?"

"You're going to clue me in on life? I'm not a Sunday school teacher, you know."

"Oh right. You're a big hotshot po—"

"Don't say it." I glanced around quickly to see who might be overhearing, but no one was within earshot. "We don't have to advertise." I stirred sugar and cream into my coffee. "It's not too late for you, Tami. You're young and could have a much better life."

"Forget it," she said. "You've made your point. But hey, don't feel sorry for me."

"I don't. I just think you're worth much more." I took a sip of coffee. Maybe it was too late for her. She didn't need a mother and I sure couldn't be one either. "Look, why did you call? Have you got what I need?"

"Wait." Now she looked all around. No one was paying any attention. She lowered her voice to just above a whisper. "This is something new—something that oughta to be worth a couple extra bucks. Stevie's got some deal going down. For tonight. It's pretty big and I just thought you might want to know about it."

I sighed. I was hoping for the final details on our dealer in the projects, but info is info. "Stevie? Is this Steve Crooks?" She nodded.

"Okay. Do you know when or where?"

"Stevie said for me to be at the Texas Star Hotel at 8:30. Some big-time suit from here in town. But he made me swear to be gone by one-thirty a.m. because he's bringing over some other V.I.P. types to meet this suit. Says he wants me gone before they show."

"Do you know who this guy is you're to meet?"

"No."

"Or who these other important guys are?"

"No, but they're from out of town, Stevie said. I'll bet they're Colombians or Jamaicans."

"What room are you supposed to go to?"

"Stevie calls me when he knows. I'll call you."

I checked my watch, 2:30 p.m. Barely enough time to get things set up if I got started now. I slid a fifty-dollar bill under the sugar bowl; if her information was righteous she'd get another fifty.

"Good work, Tami." She stuffed the money away. I told her I'd see her in a day or two. I picked up our check and hoped her information on Stevie's deal paid dividends.

"See ya later, Dirty Harriet." She gave me a lop-sided grin and a half-wave.

In May 1904, the police chief announced compliance with a city ordinance requiring new uniforms for his force. The ordinance stated: "the dress of the patrolman shall consist of a navy blue, indigo dyed sack coat with short rolling collar, to fasten at the neck and to reach half-way between the articulation of the hip joint and the knee, with four buttons on the front. The pantaloons have to have a white cord in the seam. The cap to be navy blue cloth with a light metal wreath in front." The chief instead ordered felt hats and requested helmets for foot police, making them look like "real city policemen." The police clerk refused to wear his uniform—red trousers, yellow coat, and green cap—saying it made him look like an organ-grinder's monkey. (Compiled from Austin History Center Records.)

Chapter 5

Everett "Ham" Hamilton made lieutenant at age forty. Most people would guess he's a high school math teacher instead of a police detective. The only time he looked police-like was in his dress blues uniform, but of course, he wore plain clothes mostly. A couple of inches shorter than my five feet ten and a half, he had blond hair, green eyes and a scar across his chin where he got cut by a crazed dope dealer. After that incident he became proficient in Tukong martial arts and would soon master a black belt.

Shortly after I returned to the office, Ham got back from Waco and I clued him in on Tami's tip. He thanked me and said the squad would take care of it. When I opened my mouth to protest, he said, "You're still on desk duty. I can't let you." Without drawing a breath he continued, "Besides, we can't afford for Stevie to see you with Tami."

I knew tonight would be a reconnaissance only. Just to identify the players and try to get a hint about who they were and what they were doing. I knew grumping wouldn't help, but I did it anyway.

"Don't get your britches all in a twist, okay? If the info is good you'll be back in time to help out. I only hope this is the confirmation we need on this out-of-town bunch the Feds mentioned." He gave me his sternest look.

"Okay," I said and headed back to the main building to finish my boring shift of imputing crime reports. Not my idea of police work, but it was mandatory.

I put my time in and left for home. Once there, I fed the cats, popped the top on a Diet Coke and opened my mail. A

Visa bill, an envelope proclaiming I may have already won ten million dollars—just send me the money—and the rest was more junk.

I mixed a tuna salad and opened a package of tortilla chips. I pulled on a heavy sweater, slid the glass door open and carried my food out onto the deck. Lyric came with me. Melody is a house cat and is never sure if she wants out or not, but I left the door open. Eventually, she stepped a timorous paw out and then another and soon came to hunker down near me. Lyric, equally at home inside or out, pranced around, sharpening his claws on the wooden rails that circled the deck, doing his best to show off for Melody. They both have been fixed, but he still had enough hormones left to act feline-macho sometimes.

I've tried various plants on the deck but most everything commits suicide in my care. The only luck I have is growing tomatoes. And boy I can grow those babies. But the weather hadn't been warm enough to put any plants out yet anyway. I had already decided to put out several artificial plants and pretend I had the greenest thumb of anyone around.

About two feet below the deck, the grass sloped to a jogging trail and then another tiny patch of grass before the ground dropped abruptly into the lake. Two weeping willows, a Chinese elm, and some kind of ash tree grew along the path and the bank. Besides the cat antics, I watched a jogger on the trail, two little boys fishing from a dock about a block away, and a young man sculling by in one of those long, narrow boats. They're not canoes or kayaks. I didn't know what to call them, but I get a kick out of how they glide across the lake so smoothly.

I tried to empty my mind of everything, but it didn't work today. Shooting Garcia had triggered things I'd worked hard to forget. Memories of Byron came flooding back, haunting me.

Almost eight months had passed since my husband, a man so full of life, had been destroyed. How could your world change so completely in just a blink of an eye?

Byron had been a member of APD's SWAT team, and they had been called out for a hostage situation that night. Everything went by the book until the end. The bad guy released the hostage and gave himself up and the team repacked their gear and got ready to leave.

A car suddenly careened around the corner and before Byron or anyone else could react, shots were fired. Byron still had on his bulletproof vest but had taken off his visored helmet. A bullet struck him in the head.

The drive-by had been aimed at a rival gang. Only bad timing sent them to the same corner where the SWAT team was located. Around the country, policemen sometimes get shot just for being cops, but nothing in the investigation ever showed that Byron was their target.

Byron had been rushed to Brackenridge Hospital, a super trauma center, and into surgery, but the bullet had done too much damage. The doctors said even if he ever came out of the coma he'd be paralyzed and mentally incompetent.

I had thought, finally, it would have been better all the way around if Byron had died. He hadn't and here I was, in limbo. Not married, not widowed.

Thinking about Byron reminded me of Avery Peppard again. From things he'd said I knew he still loved his wife very much. His hurt had touched some strange chord in me and I felt like weeping for him.

Love is a powerful emotion and you don't turn it off easily. But when do you give up on it? I had no answers.

A short time later, Tami came through with the hotel room number and I called it in to Lieutenant Hamilton.

I roamed the apartment for a few minutes and finally decided to go watch a basketball game. I changed into a University of Texas sweatshirt. Basketball is my all-time favorite spectator sport. Mostly women's college basketball starring the Lady Longhorns. The men's game I can take or leave.

With my height I'd played basketball in the tenth and eleventh grades in high school and was considered good enough to think I'd be offered a scholarship to the University of Texas my senior year.

Unfortunately, my smart mouth back then got me expelled my senior year. After the third time I dropped school and went to work. It didn't take long to realize the error of my ways so I took the GED and went to college.

The basketball scholarship had been lost, but love of the game was still in my blood. Besides, yelling for the home-town team and berating the referees was a great release of tensions. After a week of I.A. investigators and staring at a computer terminal for hours, I could use a stress reliever like that.

The crowd was small, our opponents weren't a big draw, so the cheerleaders in their burnt orange and white had to work extra hard to motivate people. The Lady Longhorns didn't do much to help for three quarters but finally caught fire late in the fourth quarter and won 89-75. My voice got hoarse yelling and screaming, but gosh, it felt good.

A few minutes short of midnight, I parked in the assigned space alongside my building and got out. As I strolled along the sidewalk, I paused to look up at the tiny sliver of moon with a bright star hanging under it and wished Byron were here to share the moment.

Suddenly my peripheral vision caught a flash of movement, and I saw a man sitting on the railing of my deck. He was turned halfway around, facing the lake and downtown Austin. He sat in a relaxed pose, looking for all the world like he belonged. I couldn't be certain but didn't think I recognized him.

My sneakers kept me from making any noise as I walked past my front door, staying close to the wall of the building and slid my left hand into my weapon-carry fanny pack. The Glock's reassuring weight felt good as my fingers closed around the grip. I kept my spine pressed tightly against the brick wall and when I reached the corner, I peeked around it.

A slight breeze rustled the tree leaves and ruffled my hair. The man was smoking a cigarette and when he pulled on it, I could see his profile. He gave no indication he'd seen or heard me. Now that I had a good view of him, I was sure I didn't know him.

Once he was lined up in my gun sight, I said in a normal conversational tone, "Mister, I don't know who in hell you are, but you'd better have a damn good reason for being on my deck this time of night."

In 1881, spring fever hit Austin resulting in 112 arrests—30 of them women mostly for being drunk or rowdy. The person cited and the charges (assaults, falling asleep in a public place, keeping a bawdy house, fighting, vagrancy, carrying a pistol, resisting an officer, butchering without a license) were not matched up as to who did what: 43 laborers, 4 vagrants, 3 printers, 2 trolley car drivers, 2 farmers, 2 artists, 1 newsboy, 1 express agent, 1 cowboy, 1 bartender, 1 shoemaker, 1 constable and 1 deputy sheriff were among those charged. (Compiled from: Austin History Center Records.)

Chapter 6

"Migod, woman. You scared a year's growth out of me." He turned his body and swung his legs down in order to face me.

"Slowly," I said, with the Glock still aimed at him. "Keep your hands where I can see them and tell me who you are."

"You've got to be kidding," he said, but stopped.

My complex had security lights on poles and attached to the eaves of the buildings so it was easy enough to see him. He was on the lanky side, too thin for my taste, with carroty-red hair and fair skin. He wore a western-style plaid shirt, pale blue brushed-denim pants and a darker blue Levi's jacket. "Make one sudden move, buster, and we'll see who's kidding."

"Lord, deliver me from paranoid female cops." He laughed, although it was a nervous sounding attempt. "You can put your gun away, Ms. Barrow. I'm harmless."

So, he knew my name, but what did that prove? If he were the President I would still be cautious. Single women are always vulnerable. I searched my memory, trying to place his face or put a name to it. Maybe I'd arrested him once. Nothing came to mind. I ignored his suggestion and asked, "You going to tell me who you are?"

"Jason Foxx." His voice held a smirking tone. "I'm a private dick."

I almost shot him on the spot just on principle. "I beg your pardon?"

He unfolded his long body from the top of the railing, slid his feet onto the deck and leaned back casually, elbows on the top rail. "You know—a shamus." He straightened and took a step towards me.

"Stop," I said. "Don't move 'til I tell you to move." He stopped. "Okay, turn around. Spread your legs, hands up and behind your head." Maybe he actually was Jason Foxx, private eye, but I wanted him to think twice about being so blase about being out on my deck. He could have called first or something.

"Aw, shit. This is dumb."

"Maybe, but you're on my deck. You'll have to play by my rules."

He turned slowly and assumed the position. I patted him down and not too gently either. I noted the gun holstered under his arm and asked him to take it out, slowly and drop it on the ground.

"Didn't think I needed to be armed to visit a beautiful woman but I feel undressed without it."

"Take three steps forward." When he complied, I kicked his gun off my deck and into the shrubs. Then I said, "Keep your legs spread, then with one hand, take your identification out slowly and hold it up over your head."

Using one hand, he pulled a wallet out from his back pocket, flipped it open, and held it up in the air over his shoulder.

I kept my gun in my left hand, pointed in the direction of his spinal column and took the wallet in my right. The lighting was good enough to see his official license from the Texas Board of Private Investigators. I noted his last name was spelled with a double x at the end, but details of the small photo weren't clear. Or else it wasn't a good likeness. It showed a crew cut, light-haired man.

I checked his vital statistics. The age looked right, 40, and he was listed at six feet tall, 185 pounds. His hair was definitely not the same now; it was curly and hung down over his collar in back. I couldn't tell if it was a natural curl or a perm. Other than that, as near as I could tell he pretty much matched the picture.

Ever since second grade when Lanny Joe Martin broke my heart by deciding he liked my best friend better and started walking her home every day, I've had a thing against guys with red hair. I can't help my prejudice.

"Avery Peppard hired me," Foxx said, his voice now staccato. "He told me to talk to you. If I had known it was going to be such an ordeal, I'd have told him to lump it."

"You do have a way with words, Mr. Foxx. Okay. You can turn around now but I ought to arrest you."

He turned, and I handed the wallet back to him. "What in heck did you do to your hair?"

He ignored that with a look. "Will you put that gun away, please? Guns pointed in my direction aggravate my ulcer." He motioned to my patio door. "Why don't you ask me in for coffee, and I'll explain why I'm here?"

I relaxed and put the Glock back into my fanny pack. "I don't think so. It's late and I have to work tomorrow."

"Aw, hell. That coffee spiel always works for that guy on that coffee commercial, why it doesn't it work for me?"

I couldn't help myself, I laughed. "Maybe he says it with more panache." It would be tacky to mention the guy on TV was a hunk and he wasn't.

"Guess I'd better practice sincerity. Do you think you might have some free time tomorrow to talk about Mr. Peppard?"

Oh, well. Peppard wouldn't have sent the guy over if it weren't important. But I hadn't lied when I said I'd be tied up all day tomorrow. Plans were in place to meet my parents for brunch and I knew their question and answer session would take up most of the day. Looks like I had no choice. "Maybe we should talk tonight. Come on in."

Foxx walked behind me, scrounged his gun from the flowerbed and followed me inside.

The cats were waiting to greet me, but as soon as Melody spied Jason Foxx, she ran into the bedroom to hide. Lyric, who isn't exactly shy, surprised me by promptly flopping down, belly-up, on Foxx's black suede Hushpuppies, wanting his tummy scratched. Usually he's a little more stand-offish.

"Hey, Kitty," said Foxx, reaching down and letting Lyric smell his hand and fingers before rubbing them along the cat's stomach.

Well, well, I thought. A cat person. Man can't be all bad. "That's Lyric," I told Foxx. "Melody was the shy one who streaked past a moment ago, heading for a safe place under the bed. Have a seat and I'll make some coffee. Or would you rather join me in having a beer?"

"Beer would be great." Foxx sat down on the charcoal gray Hide-A-Bed sofa I'd bought second-hand, and Lyric hopped right up into the man's lap.

"You might want to make Lyric get down," I said, walking to the kitchen. "He sheds and even worse, has a tendency to drool when you pet him." I got the beer and asked. "Do you want a glass?"

"No way, a glass only warms it up too quickly."

I handed a can and a paper coaster to Foxx and sat opposite him in a platform rocker.

He put the beer on an end table and, after scratching under Lyric's chin several more times, placed the cat on the floor. Lyric came over and started to plop on my sneaker. "You've had some attention already, you fickle feline." I slipped my foot out, no easy feat with the laces tied, and Lyric settled in as he dearly loves to stick his nose into my yucky shoes—why is beyond me.

I popped open my can. "What do you think of Peppard's story?"

"A little bizarre, but believable. Poor guy is scared out of his gourd. I guess he's got a good reason."

"Scared? Has something else happened?"

"He claims someone is stalking him, but he can't prove it. I mean, he doesn't even have a coherent car description." Foxx took a drink.

"What do you think, Mr. Foxx? Have you seen a stalker?"

"Call me Jason," he said. "And may I call you Zoe?"

I nodded, picked up my sneaker, untied it and put it back on, leaving the lace loose.

"I only met the man for the first time earlier tonight," he said. "Thought I'd better talk to you and see what your thinking was."

So had Peppard actually sent Foxx over here or not? "Tell me a little about yourself, Mr., er, Jason."

"I'm from Houston. Worked at Houston Police Department until about a year ago. Got my private ticket and moved to Austin last summer when my divorce was final. A friend of mine referred me to two attorneys here. One, a Ms. Bethany Radcliff, I think you know."

I knew Bethany slightly. She's Lianne's sister. A sharp, tough lady.

Foxx continued. "I met Kyle Raines through Ms. Radcliff."

"By the way," I said, "sorry about the earlier hostility. Think I'm a little paranoid lately."

"I understand. I read about your recent trouble."

I didn't want to discuss such things with Mr. Foxx. "How do you plan to help Peppard?"

"Follow at a discreet distance. Hope I spot someone stalking him. Identify who it is."

"I think following the missus to identify the boyfriend would be smart."

He slapped his forehead. "Why didn't I think of that?" His voice held that smirking tone again.

"You've already assigned someone to Mrs. Peppard. Do you have a partner?"

"No. Just a rent-a-cop. But what I was thinking—I mean, I heard you were at loose ends—desk duty or something. If you'd like to keep an eye on Peppard, then I could keep an eye on the missus."

"I'm going back on duty soon."

"Then just until you do. I can pay you," he said with a faint smile. "Besides, two heads are better than the proverbial one."

"No. I think not. And as delightful as this has all been I do have a full schedule tomorrow and need some rest."

"You're kicking me out? Damn," he said, putting down his can. "Thought I was making points here."

"Points?"

"I was thinking about asking you to dinner tomorrow night."

"I already said I've got a busy day. Besides, I don't date."

"You don't—"

I stood and interrupted, everything perfectly clear now. This idiot knew I was a woman alone, and probably thought I was desperate. "Look, Mr. Foxx. I don't know what's on your mind, but forget it. I'm not available." I walked with my shoelace flapping and stood with my hand on the doorknob.

"Let me make amends," he said as my telephone rang.

I let it ring and waited for him to go.

"You'd better answer," he said, glancing at his watch.

"After midnight. It's likely to be important."

I didn't know which grated me most, the insistent ringing or the insistent private investigator. I halfway pushed him out the door and headed for the counter dividing my kitchen from the living room and picked up the receiver.

Ryan Watkins, an evening dispatcher at Austin police communications was on the line. "Is this Zoe Barrow?"

I assured him it was.

"Kyle Raines asked me to call. Said tell you they found Tami Louise's body in a room at the Star Hotel. Her throat's been cut."

A police blotter in 1953 revealed 20 arrests and 84 complaints filed over a week's period. The kingpin of prostitution was also arrested. He supposedly furnished hotel porters, cab drivers and bellhops with "girls for dates." (Compiled from: Austin History Center Records.)

Chapter 7

Foxx insisted on driving me saying I looked quite upset. After saying thanks, he made record time and I left him in the hotel lobby.

The Star is built like a four-pointed star with a round atrium in the center. Byron and I had met here often for fajitas and drinks. I'd only been back once since his accident; that time to meet Tami. The central portion rises one story taller than the hotel's fourteen floors and houses a pricey restaurant, which slowly revolves three hundred sixty degrees each hour.

Live trees, shrubs and plants grow everywhere. Fountains and waterfalls babble and streams run all through the ground floor which is mainly an open bar area. Sofas and chairs and tables are grouped for conversation areas.

Exotic birds live in huge gilded cages among the trees and plants. Mahogany banisters ring each floor's level and seasonal blooming plants fill planters at regular intervals along the mezzanine-like hallways. The planters also trail ivy along and over the rails. With the macaw's cries and the babbling brook you soon think you're in a jungle. Tami liked the hotel but it wasn't discreet enough to meet an informant.

I remembered her saying how she liked standing at the banisters and looking down onto lobby/bar to people watch. "But the best part is, you can watch people go up and down in those glass walled elevators," she'd grinned.

I knew that people inside those elevators often acted as if they couldn't be seen; they'd kiss and fondle one another, women check their hair and make-up, men rearrange their jockey shorts, kids pick their noses or hassle each other, both males and females scratch their asses, and couples would argue. "Sometimes it is more fun than a three-ring circus," Tami had said.

I spotted a patrol officer near the reception desk, flashed my badge and he told me to meet Kyle Raines on the tenth floor.

I tried to remember how easily I could be seen in this glass cage and conduct myself properly, but I caught myself reaching into the neck of my sweatshirt and pulling up my bra strap when I momentarily forgot. I glanced around guiltily and knew someone, somewhere saw me even if I didn't see them.

Lianne Crowder and Kyle Raines were outside the door of room 1037. That room, along with three others, are somewhat hidden because they're located across the hallway and behind the backside of the elevator wall. Directly across from each room are the ice and vending machines, and the housing for the elevator shafts.

The door to 1037 was open and a myriad of officers, both uniformed and plain clothes, milled about inside. Flashbulbs were flashing and fingerprint techs were brushing, taping and lifting prints, while other people talked or wrote notes. All doing whatever was necessary to preserve and record the crime scene.

Kyle was dressed in khaki pants and an open black windbreaker, which revealed a striped knit shirt. His beard looked wild and more bushy than ever as if he hadn't combed or trimmed it in days and a Dallas Cowboy baseball cap was perched bill to the back on his head. Haute couture of an undercover cop.

"Cute outfit, dude," I said to Kyle to break the tension I felt. I turned to my friend. "Lianne, I didn't expect to see you here." She was currently assigned to vice.

"I came over when I heard; I've known Tami for several years."

"I'd forgotten. You busted her the first time, didn't you?"

"She was only seventeen back then."

A male voice called Lianne from inside, so she entered the room.

I looked at Kyle. "This isn't the room where Tami was supposed to be, is it?"

"She went to room 1204 at 8:30 p.m., as planned, came out at 11:00 and left the hotel."

"You saw her leave?"

"I didn't actually see her drive away. Steve Crooks and these dudes showed up. I reported their descriptions to Ham just as Tami got into her car and started the engine."

"You were outside?"

He nodded. "Standing behind a charter bus and trying to look like I was checking the tires.

"Then the Lieutenant got all excited," Kyle continued, "and I quit watching Tami."

"Oh? What thrilled Ham?" Our boss, "Ham" Hamilton, wasn't the excitable type.

"You know that Jamaican ring he's been trying to get a line on?"

I nodded.

"These dudes here tonight looked like the real McCoy. I figured if they were, we were gonna be in tall cotton with the drug task force."

"So you let Tami go?" My voice sounded accusatory but I couldn't help it.

"What was I supposed to do?" He scratched his cheek and pulled on the beard. "We were there to identify these guys. Tami wasn't needed anymore. And it looked like she was leaving."

Kyle was right. Surveillance to identify these out-of-town guys was the team's mission. Not to keep an eye on Tami. She told us what was going on and that ended her task from our standpoint.

"And you have no idea why she came back?" I asked. It was crazy—the place was surrounded by cops and my snitch gets killed. "Or who cut her throat?"

"Zoe, it's got to be totally unrelated. Maybe someone saw her when she first came in, figured she was a hooker and waited for her outside."

I took a couple of deep breaths. "Sorry Kyle. I know there was nothing you could have done, but why was she back inside?"

"Maybe somebody made her an offer and they went upstairs," Kyle said. "Later they got into an argument or once she got upstairs with him, maybe he got nasty and she refused him. Whatever. The guy got mad and offed her."

"Who is the room registered to?"

"No one. This room was supposed to be empty."

Lianne joined us. "I need the whole story here, Kyle, my old partner caught the case and needs my help." She pulled out a notebook. "Who called this in?"

"Security got a report about a horrible fight going on in this room," he said. "A woman supposedly was screaming bloody murder in there." His nod indicating the crime scene room. "But when the security guards got here, everything was quiet. They listened at the door and didn't hear anything. Knocked, but didn't get a response. They called the desk and the room wasn't rented. They figured the screams came from some drunken tourists down the hall someplace. Their chief was off having dinner somewhere and they waited until he got back before reporting to him."

Kyle continued, "When the security honcho came up with

his two guards and couldn't get a response, he opened the door. They found Tami and called 911. Dispatch put it over the radio and I picked it up. Since I was already here, I—"

"I can't believe no one popped the door. Doesn't make sense. If they had, they might have prevented this. Damn, and double damn," I said. "Where was the rest of the team?"

"Bubba was still staked out outside and Krantz was up on the twelfth floor. They'd already reported earlier that the lights had gone out in Room 1203. Ham had said it looked like those guys were settled in for the night, and for everyone except Bubba and Krantz to go home."

"Wait a minute, Kyle. Steve Crooks and the two Jamaicans were spending the night in Room 1203? The one next door to the one registered to Stevie's pal?"

"It sounds confusing until you know the setup. I understand from the security chief that 1204 is the parlor of an executive suite, 1205 is a bedroom, with king bed. Room 1203 is a connecting bedroom with two double beds and you can rent the whole thing as a two-bedroom deluxe suite. That's what Stevie's guy did. Just rented the whole thing."

"So there's no reason to suspect these hot-shot dudes you were watching?" Lianne wanted to know. "I mean, your guy didn't see anyone leave from up there?"

"No. Krantz was watching both doors. No one left or entered after Crooks and his guys went inside."

The homicide investigator called out for Lianne to come back inside and she said, "Sorry to interrupt, Kyle." She motioned to me. "Zoe, you want to take a look see before they take her out?"

Pure dread filled me. Tami and I saw each other on the average of once a week. We had a weird relationship. You can't be friends with your snitch but in many ways you're like an older relative—an aunt or a cousin. You give them advice.

You listen to their troubles, you share the good things that happen to them along with the bad. A certain amount of personality comes into play. Yours and your informant's.

Tami was bubbly and funny and vulnerable all at the same time. She was also a hooker and an ex-drug user with a police record. Her world was totally different from mine, but we had a connection.

I hated going in, yet I felt an obligation to this girl who'd been part of my life for nearly two years. To see what had been done to her. To become angry at what had happened. I would give the homicide investigators all I could to help them find her killer.

"Sure, Lianne," I said. "Thanks."

My eyes were riveted immediately on the girl lying crosswise on the bed. I noticed Tami's hands had already been placed in paper bags to preserve any evidence that might be found. Sometimes movie or television cops use plastic bags but that's a big no-no in real life. Plastic facilitates the growth of bacteria and destroys evidence. Half on her side and topless, her orangey-red ponytail dangled below the mattress. Her right arm was by her side and the left flung up near her head. Her legs were bent slightly at the knees. A black lace bra puddled on the floor alongside a pair of four-inch stiletto heel white shoes.

It wasn't Tami. Her bubbly personality was missing, her essence was gone—the human shell, which housed her in life, was the only thing left.

"Do we have *anything?*" I asked Lianne.

"A little crud under the fingernails."

"Maybe she scratched him."

"One can always hope." Lianne paused and looked at me. "Are you okay?"

Turning away and taking a deep breath, I answered, "I'm

fine." I looked around the room and spotted Tami's clothes hanging in the closet. Had she known her killer, or was he just some guy who'd wanted a quick lay and somehow things got out of hand? If she didn't know him, why were her clothes hung up so neatly? "Anything else, Lianne?"

"Looks like he used a scalpel-sharp knife, from what I could see; maybe a switchblade. Forensics can probably identify the type used. We won't know about secretions until the doc checks, but I'd bet a week's pay she had recently had sex."

"Even if her killer didn't mess with her, Lianne, she was in Room 1204 from 8:30 until 11 p.m," I said. "I don't think she was up there to watch MTV." I hadn't realized how harsh my voice sounded until Lianne's head snapped around to look at me.

"Take it easy, Zoe. I'm on your side."

"Sorry. Guess seeing her like this upset me more than I realized."

Lianne's green eyes glanced around the room. "We dusted, but there's probably forty prints in here, mostly smudged from the maids cleaning. If we ever get a viable suspect, maybe he'll match one of them."

The technicians from the medical examiner's office had that bored look as if waiting for us to finish. I walked back to the bed and looked at Tami Louise once more. Was it only this afternoon when I saw her? Less than twelve hours ago she'd been in awe of my killing Garcia.

A gun for protection, she'd said. I remembered how I'd almost laughed in her face. She wanted a gun and only hours later she is killed. Maybe she could have shot her assailant; maybe not. The gun probably would have been in her purse anyway and of no use whatsoever.

She'd given me info to set up a surveillance and she would

have kept her date with Stevie even if I hadn't known about it. This had been a routine job with no premonition of danger so I couldn't put a guilt trip on myself. Yet I felt guilty.

According to Kyle, Tami had completed the job for Stevie, had completed the job for us and was basically in her car to leave. Who or what had lured her back inside? Did she come willingly with someone she knew or was it just a spur of the moment thing? How did they get into this room? Many questions but no answers. Hotels and ladies of the evening manage to work in tandem ever since the first inns were built, I imagine. But this hotel had a lot to answer for in my book.

I remembered suggesting to her that she go back to school while she was still young enough to make something out of herself. I had wanted to shake some sense into her. I had wanted her off the streets.

Well, she was off the streets now.

In 1955 the Austin city council decided police officers had better things to do than monitor parking meters and thus the parkaidette division of APD was born. Qualifications for these female paragons of virtue were: 25-35 yrs., 5'2"-5'8". Have good speech, poise, tact, diplomacy, attitude, appearance, temperament, acceptable penmanship and be married. Preferably with children, husbands should be permanently employed (but not by the city) and not transients with the armed forces or a student at the university. (Compiled from: Austin History Center Records.)

Chapter 8

"Zoe Barrow, meet Sergeant Investigator Harry Albright." Lianne and I stood in the hallway on the tenth floor of the hotel near the elevators, when a man joined us.

Albright was big, at least six feet, four or five inches and weighed close to two hundred-seventy pounds. If Kyle Raines looked bear-like, this guy looked gorilla-like—I'm talking huge. His face was weathered and in his hazel eyes a wearied look shown through. His light brown hair revealed no gray, but the lines on his face said late forties. His nose matched the rest of his size, normal-sized ears, which lay back against his head, and full lips. He didn't look particularly happy to meet me, but then he surprised me.

"I'm pleased to shake the hand of Zoe Barrow. Nice job on taking down Garcia." His voice was a deep baritone and stern sounding, although his words were a compliment.

I nodded. Here's a question for Emily Post: how to respond politely to congratulations for killing someone?

"I was Lopez's training officer," he continued. "Good man. I hear he'll have full recovery."

"That *is* good news," I said.

Albright let his eyes stray to Lianne and his demeanor softened. It wasn't the first time I'd seen the effect my friend had on males. With her abundant auburn curls and sparkling green eyes, men often just start to drool.

A Castilian Spanish grandmother gave her face an exotic look and she's built like Raquel Welch—which she maintains with workouts a couple of times a week. It's enough to make me give up Häagen-Dazs for life. But I don't. It takes a lot to

My sister-in-law Pat called; she's married to my younger brother, Herbert Taylor, Jr., better known as Chip. "If your mom hears about this she's going to have a hissy fit." My mom thinks being a police officer is much too dangerous, and the idea of me in a shoot-out would renew her pressure on me to resign. She'd never liked me in blue, either.

Fortunately, my folks were on vacation in Puerto Vallarta. "Don't I know." The picture of my mother when she did find out was not a pretty one. "How did you find out, by the way?"

"The paper said an off-duty cop returning from a basket-ball game was involved in the shooting of one Jesse Garcia. Since me and you and Chip were at the game last night and if another female cop had attended you would have introduced her, I put two and two together."

"Will Chip tell Mom if she calls?"

"Of course not silly. We know how she is."

Pat said to call if I needed anything. When I hung up, I breathed a thank you to the vacation Gods who'd lured my parents away at such an opportune time.

Since they had allowed me to sleep late, Lyric and Melody began showing off, wanting my attention. I laughed at their shenanigans and spent the better part of an hour teasing them with a catnip mouse on a string. I stroked and petted and brushed them, and they made me feel enough better to try eating a second piece of toast. This time it stayed down.

My pal, Lianne, came a few minutes later. If she wasn't such a good friend, I'd have hated her because of her drop-dead looks and body to match. She's assigned to homicide because of her undercover successes in vice. She gave me a quick hug and asked if I had any coffee.

Lianne followed me down the hall and I assured her I was doing fine. My kitchen reminds me of my grandmother Taylor's kitchen in Fort Worth. It's long and somewhat narrow, myself out and decided to go back to college that he asked me for a date. From that time on, we were inseparable and whatever he did, I wanted to be a part of and that included the Austin police department.

"Byron always appreciated lovely women."

"Do you know Byron well?"

Peppard began shaking his head. "Not the adult Byron. He was still in his late teens the last time I saw him."

"Well, Byron would marry the woman he loved, no matter what physical attributes she had."

"Sounds like he's more like Levi than Jean. How in the world did that happen?"

I smiled. Peppard knew the Barrows quite well. Levi Barrow is a fantastic person and Byron was much like his father. My *mother-in-law*, however, was another story. Jean Barrow acted as if "what will people think" was of the utmost importance, especially when it related to her son. About the only reason she tolerated me was because she thought I was suitably attractive and came from fairly decent bloodlines— like a cow or something. Byron, his father and I had laughed about her attitude many times. "Yes, he is like . . . was . . . whatever."

"I'm sorry," Avery said. "I've heard the sad news of Byron's accident. And please forgive my making assumptions about you or your husband."

The waiter appeared just then with the wine, interrupting our conversation. During the ritual of opening the bottle and pouring the symbolic first taste for Avery, I spent the time scrutinizing him. After noting the lines around his eyes and on his forehead, I revised my earlier estimate of his age upward a bit. He still looked good despite the addition.

"I appreciate your taking the time to meet tonight," Peppard said. "Time could be crucial. Strangely enough, uh . . .

you two have nothing better to do, I could really use some help tonight."

Lianne and I knew the first hours of a homicide were important, official assignments could be sorted out later.

"Let's start by talking to everyone again, the security folks and the people who heard the screams. The patrol officers did a room-to-room for an eye-witness." He pulled a small spiral notebook and pen out of his shirt pocket. "Two thought they saw someone and they're waiting. Let's don't disturb the others again tonight. If we need to later, we've got names and addresses. And we still need to search Miss Smuts's apartment."

I liked the way he called Tami "Miss Smuts."

"Okay," I said. "Questioning first?" Harry nodded.

We questioned the guests who'd heard any noise from Room 1037 and the ones who thought they had seen something, in short order.

Lianne and I sat opposite and each person we interrogated sat at one end. Albright stood over by the windows facing us and the table. He let Lianne lead the questions, with me backing her up. He only interrupted for clarification or when he specifically wanted to know something. This wasn't a bad cop/good cop routine, just a straight search for any clue.

We talked to the witnesses and then got ready for the hotel crew.

"I find it unbelievable the security guards acted like they did," said Lianne. "Why didn't they just go on into that room where the screams reportedly came from?"

We brought them in one at a time. I thought they looked like Tweedle-dee and Tweedle-dum—blond, blue-eyed, preppy-handsome, even their looks were interchangeable. Both guards swore they had not heard anything suspicious while standing outside room 1037. I wondered if their brains were also interchangeable.

"They're just college students, Li. They're part-timers. They punch a time clock and then hope for some study time," I said. "They are not very imaginative or responsible."

Richard Hebron, the security chief, stacked up different. "I'm forty-five years old," he said. He looked ten years younger. His kind of face would still look young at sixty-five. I judged him to be about five-feet eleven, weighing one-eighty to one-ninety. Muscular but wiry, with reddish blond hair and blue-green eyes. His front lower teeth were in desperate need of braces and he had a air of cockiness, but despite that, some women probably considered him attractive. He recited the facts in an articulate and precise manner to Lianne, ignoring me totally. I was used to it.

"What I'd like to know," I asked, "is how did Tami and her killer get into this supposedly vacant room?"

"Good question. I'm afraid I don't have any good answers," Hebron said, with a quick glance at me. "I mean, there are several good answers, but I just don't know which is the correct one."

"Why don't you try some out?" I asked.

Hebron had trouble tearing his eyes away from Lianne long enough to look at me. In my book he was mentally undressing her, and the smirk I saw on her face meant she realized it and would try to work it to her advantage.

His look to me said he was humoring me. "Since the hotel stopped using keys and started using computer cards, it isn't easy to pop a room. Someone could always ask a desk clerk for a spare card and get one, however. The clerks are supposed to ask for ID, but some of these kids aren't too conscientious about it."

Harry Albright spoke up. "Obviously, a good cat burglar can open any door in about ten seconds flat."

"Right," said Hebron, looking up at Harry. "We don't get many burglars around here, but it could happen. Or you pretend to a maid you've left your key inside and get her to unlock the door. Everyone seen that happened in movies or TV."

"Once it's open," said Albright, "a piece of tape across the lock would do the trick."

"This room's location," I said, "makes it easy, too. Hidden away like it is."

Hebron rubbed his nose and put a wry smile on his mouth. "What we're talking about here is someone using the room for a quick piece—excuse me, ladies—all he wants is to do his business and get out."

"So you think that's why someone broke into this room?" I asked.

"No. I think he popped open Room 1037 for dealing," said Hebron. He wore a sincere smile, looking at me but it didn't quite reach his eyes. "I think the guy was selling and the hooker showed up. He's got this great setup—a pad bought and paid for by his dealer and so this cat takes advantage."

When his eyes slid off mine, I got that weird feeling I often get when someone is lying to me. It's not totally infallible and I can't completely explain it. It's a funny sort of tingle, almost like an itch at the base of my spine. When it happens, I try to pay attention to every word that person says. Because they're lying or not telling everything they know. I concentrated on his words and his body language as he continued.

I wondered why would he so readily admit to drug dealing going on here in his hotel?

Lianne asked. "If that's true, then why was Tami lured back? She was seen in her car."

"I don't know," said Hebron. "Maybe they had prior business—his or hers? He saw her, flagged her down and she couldn't refuse him?"

"Tami's a working girl. She wouldn't do anything for free," said Lianne.

"Right. Maybe he offered her a bonus or something."

"But then why kill her? That doesn't make sense," I said.

"She made him mad about something—women like to do that, you know—tease a guy until he goes nuts." Hebron's tone changed to disgust. "Most likely she went upstairs, got him all hot and bothered then wouldn't come across."

"Cheap bastard probably refused to pay," said Lianne.

I said, "Tami never was one to be pushed around. So, you think she got into an argument and this yahoo went berserk?"

"I'm sure you're right," said Hebron.

He seemed terribly eager for us to adopt his theory—even admitting the possibility of drug dealers having a free rein here. Maybe now he hoped his cooperation would keep us from reporting his slackness to his boss.

Albright thanked Hebron and said we'd need a formal statement from him early tomorrow.

"The hotel hopes we can clear this up quick so as to minimize any adverse publicity," he said as he stood. "Other troubles have happened here and we can't afford to let this hang over our heads too long. The only good thing is she was a local—not a tourist or a conventioneer."

"You're all heart." The words popped out before I thought.

"Hey, I didn't mean anything. Broad was just a hooker."

I stood and probably would have punched him right then, but Harry Albright had turned the guy around and ushered him out before I could clear my chair.

Albright came back and began to pace. "That guy's hiding something," he said. "Dealers popping doors and selling drugs and he don't see nothing. Won't surprise me if he's taking a hefty cut on the side."

"That's probably why those kids didn't pop that door. Hebron's business and they were to stay out of it."

Harry grunted, stopped. "I'm gonna need some computer work, too. Sort the files on dealers who have a record of sexual assaults. Focus on ones who like knives and who work this part of town. So much crime, so little time," he muttered in a stage whisper and began to pace once again.

"Go on and get the computer work started," I said. "Lianne and I'll go to Tami's place and give it the once-over."

"Are you sure you want to do this, Zoe?" His voice had gone back his stern mode. "It's late and you're not back on the clock yet."

"Look, I'll be willing to work on my own time; if you'll let me. I want to know who killed Tami. It's important to me."

Harry Albright got a funny look on his face. "I want the bastard, too." His voice husky. "I don't like young women getting killed in my town." He didn't speak for a moment and when he did the gruffness was gone. "I appreciate your help."

Before I could answer, Harry Albright was gone.

"What's the deal with him?" I asked.

"Harry probably wishes for the good old days when female officers were meter maids and nothing more. They used to call them parkaidettes he told me once, but he knows now how much he needs us. Anything else you'll find out as you get to know him better."

It was three a.m. when Lianne and I woke up the manager at Tami's apartment. "Apartment" was a reach—a South Congress motel that went bust and reopened as weekly rent-a-rooms with kitchenettes. The Bye and Bye Motel sign was hand-painted, faded and peeling. A skuzzy-looking place.

The manager said her name was Miss Winslow, emphasis

on the Miss, when she finally opened the door. She looked as if she tipped the scales at three-hundred-plus pounds and her hair was gray and matted on one side. Sweat rolled down her sixtyish-looking face and into the creases of her triple chins, even though the early morning was cool enough for a jacket. Her chenille robe was gray, too, but I think it had originally been white. She wasn't happy, but I hadn't expected her to be.

Number six was on the same side as the manager's and only a few doors down, so we left the car parked where it was, opposite the office, and just walked over.

Lianne opened the door into one large room. A combination living room/bedroom with a sort of alcove for a kitchenette. The bathroom was separate. The walls were grime streaked and pocked with nail holes and maybe once painted a blue color but impossible to tell for certain. The bed had faded floral sheets, although they looked clean, and no bedspread. A pale green thermal blanket lay folded at the foot.

Tami had made an attempt to decorate. The blue miniblinds looked new on the curtainless windows. A sixteen-by-twenty inch portrait of Elvis, painted on black velvet, hung on one wall over the sofa. A nightstand held a goose-necked lamp, a chest of drawers and a vanity—all of which were freshly painted white.

Not such a bad room I thought, just depressing.

"You start in here," said Lianne, "I'll check the bathroom and kitchen area."

"Why do you get the easy part?"

"I'm senior."

"Senior, my eye," I said. "We rank the same."

"But I'm older."

"Only by six weeks." Lianne was born January ninth and I was born February twenty-fifth. "Looking for anything specific?" I pulled on a pair of latex gloves and watched Lianne do the same.

"Address or trick book." She walked into the bathroom. "Any letters or notes from someone making a threat or an implied threat. The usual."

Everything was tidy, and when I opened the closet door I immediately saw where most of Tami's money went since she cleaned up from drugs. Her flashy hooker clothing was most prominent, but a few items of quality from the better department stores filled the remainder. The good stuff was for dressing as a regular person. Shoes stacked on the shelf above were mostly spike-heeled and bright colors. No boxes or suitcases or cartons inside, only clothes and shoes.

Tami tried to make a real home out of this little pathetic place, I thought, as I walked to the chest of drawers. Surfaces were uncluttered and dust-free. I couldn't help thinking how I'd hate for anyone to come in and go through my apartment.

The top drawer held a beaded evening bag, costume jewelry and a glove assortment used for role-playing with her customers. Good quality underwear: bras, sexy nightgowns, teddies and assorted lingerie from Victoria's Secret and hosiery in the second. The third held sweaters, blouses, shirts and T-shirts. Everything was folded neatly and it only took a moment to feel underneath to discover nothing here either.

Lianne came out of the bathroom. "Tami practiced safe sex. I found condoms and she also took birth control pills. Find anything?"

"Nope."

We walked to the kitchenette. A small refrigerator, a hot plate, and a sink were crammed against one wall. The sink was small and yellow. A pot of ivy rested on a round chrome dinette table in the corner with two card-table chairs. A potholder/dishtowel set with a matching vegetable print hung on the rack by the sink.

"Shouldn't take long," I said.

"The flour canister or the bean jar maybe?"

"Or a coffee can. Tami would do something like that. I need to finish up in the bedroom."

Leaving Lianne to her task I walked back to the main living area and over to the nightstand. A small drawer was at the top and a larger one at the bottom with two bookcase-type shelves in the space between. On the top shelf, eight or ten romance novels stood on end, flanked by one sci-fi written by Isaac Asimov. I pulled them out and did a quick flip through the pages. In the Asimov book I found a photo of Tami and an older couple standing in front of a clapboard house. Tami looked about twelve. The couple looked as if the weight of the world sat on top of their heads and Tami wasn't smiling. On the back was written in blue ink: Mamma, Daddy and Me. 8929 Yale, Lubbock.

She'd never mentioned her parents and I'd assumed they were dead. And maybe they were, but we'd have to make an attempt to locate and notify them. I placed the photo on the bed before replacing the books.

The bottom drawer held a large tube of KY jelly, two vibrators, some scented oils and other paraphernalia of the prostitute's trade. No surprise there but still sad.

"All riiiight," Lianne said. She came over holding a package wrapped in aluminum foil. "Found her trick book. In the freezer."

"That's our Tami." I laughed as Lianne held the small, dark green address book outstretched on the palm of her hand. For a couple of seconds it stayed open on the first page and I read—AUVY@WORK—written in large red letters. A local phone number was written after the name in black ink in small numerals and something about the number seemed familiar. Before I had a chance to think about it Lianne flipped through the pages.

"The freezer, huh?" I asked and picked up two rolls of undeveloped film I'd found in the nightstand drawer and placed them in an evidence bag. "I'll bet that's where she kept her stash when she was on drugs."

"The foil-wrapped book was in a freezer bag," Lianne said, "with a T-bone steak."

"Not too original, but effective. Find any dope?"

"No, nothing else." Lianne looked more closely at a couple of other pages. "Hey, here's Judge Martell's number, and doesn't Tony Aldo own that new camper-trailer store? Tami's moved up in the world since I talked to her last."

"Her appeal worked in her favor—even if she didn't have the polish to be a high-class girl. She'd come a long way from being a street hooker."

Lianne closed the book. "You found anything?"

"An old photo. It might help us come up with her family. I also found some exposed film along with a bunch of letters and business papers in the vanity I need to wade through. Nothing exciting, so far."

"It's after four a.m. Let's pack it up and get home."

As she turned back to the kitchenette, I said, "Wonder who Auvy is? And why does he rate big red letters?"

"No telling but probably hung like a bull," she said.

"Give me a break. A hooker who cares about something like that? Maybe," I said, "it's just someone who always pays top dollar."

"Speaking of money. She didn't have a pimp, did she?"

"She never had what you'd call a real pimp. Just Stevie, Steve Crooks. When she first started he'd send her to guys he knew and he took a cut. But he didn't even do that the past several months because she had a lot of regulars."

"Yeah, I know Stevie," Lianne said. "Fairly decent. Not your typical pimp, although I've *never* seen many pimps in Austin, most girls are independent."

"Stevie's the one who asked her to meet these guys at the Texas Star."

"I better remember to remind Harry," she said. "He'll need to question Crooks. Could there be a motive there?"

"Possibly, but she'd already left Stevie's pals." As I riffled through papers: bills, bank statements, receipts and letters, I found two birthday cards from someone calling herself Aunt Callie. The return address was a location in Houston so I added them to the little pile of things on the bed and put them in a baggy and into my backpack.

A few minutes later we walked out. Lianne carried Tami's book. I shivered in the dampness and waited while Lianne dropped the key to Tami's place in Miss Winslow's mail slot.

The sky was overcast, without a moon. Light pollution from the stores and strip-centers along the street washed the sky a murky yellowish-pink color. I didn't notice how much darker it was. Nothing was on my mind except getting home, taking a hot shower and crawling into bed.

Lianne was on the driver's side, reaching out to unlock the door of her car, and I was on the passenger side, close to the rear fender. God, he was fast.

I didn't even see where he came from—maybe from behind the old VW van parked next to Lianne's car. Maybe from around the corner of the building.

He was just there, suddenly. A dark blur beside Lianne.

I saw his arm moving towards her. I heard his hand connect with her skull, a sickening sound, then she fell with a thud.

He turned. He wore black pants and a black jacket.

Nothing identifiable. I remembered thinking how gross and distorted a head looked with a ski mask over it.

I clawed at my backpack. My gun was inside in my carry-case. I lunged in his direction.

He was too quick. His right arm went up high and came down hard as he tried to sap me with the blackjack.

I stepped my right foot back and turned slightly to my left into him. His blow missed my head, but hit my shoulder. That whole side went numb.

I reached for my gun with my left hand. But the pain in my right shoulder and the awkwardness of my position did nothing to help. I kicked out at his knee but only grazed it.

He shoved me hard with one gloved hand. I sailed backwards and landed on my butt. A nerve shock ran down my leg, and sharp pain in my tailbone sent stars before my eyes.

Holding Tami's trick book in his hand, he rounded the corner of the manager's office, and kept going.

By then, I was on my hands and knees, gagging. I shook my head to clear the dizziness and that made it worse momentarily. I tried to move forward after him.

A car door slammed and an engine started. I lifted up on one hand and both feet and scrabbled bear-like to the corner of the building.

I blinked my eyes rapidly to clear the spinning pinpoints of light in front of my eyes. When I could focus, I saw a red and white pick-up truck. Then it sped underneath a street light, careened around a corner and out of sight. The license plate was either missing or blacked-out.

When my feet got me upright finally, I felt dizzy again and had to lean over, hands on my knees as I took some long deep breaths.

I hobbled around the car and found Lianne—breathing, but unconscious.

A door opened behind me and Miss Winslow called out. "What's all that racket out here? You want me to call the cops?"

"Call 911. Tell them. Officer needs assistance." I sat beside Lianne and took her hand.

In 1902, the Daughters of Charity were asked by the citizens of Austin to open a hospital. The Daughters, which were founded in 1633, opened the 40-bed Seton Infirmary to care for the poor and sick. The beds now number over 500 and offer a variety of health care services. (Compiled from: the Seton Hospital volunteer brochure.)

Chapter 9

"I still don't have an ID on who, but Peppard's definitely being tailed," said Jason Foxx.

"What do you mean you don't have an ID?" I asked. "Oh, you want me to run his license through motor vehicles and get a name for you?"

We were in Room 338 of Seton Hospital and it was ten minutes before noon. I was in a hospital bed and Foxx leaned upright against the wall.

At five a.m. with a severely bruised right shoulder and coccyx bone—nothing broken—and with pain medicine inside, my protest against admission had not been heeded.

Lianne had a concussion from the blow to the head by the blackjack and she would stay in the hospital for at least another day. The emergency room doctor told me they wanted to run some tests on her but mostly they wanted to keep her under observation.

This morning I convinced the doctor to release me and was almost ready to check out of my expensive accommodations when Foxx showed up. He said he'd called my office and Kyle Raines told him what had happened. I wasn't particularly glad to see him.

"No. I already found out the car was a rental. I've got a description on him from the rental agency but it's too vague. I hired a guy today who is going to try for a photo." He sat down and slouched one leg over the arm of the visitor's chair. "Honest, I was worried and came by to see how you were."

"Well, I'm doing fine." I'd be even finer if he'd leave, especially since I wore only a silly hospital gown. "In fact, I'm

96

ready to blow this joint," I said, hoping he'd take the hint.

Jason made no attempt to move. "Do you need a ride home?"

I realized for the first time that I did. Lianne and I had taken her car when we went to toss Tami's place at the Bye and Bye Motel. "You don't have to . . ."

"No problem. I'm free for the next couple of hours anyway."

He still made no attempt to move. "Okay," I said, "but you can leave now and let me change."

He waggled his eyebrows at me, slowly got up from the chair as if it took great effort, and ambled to the door. He paused. "Do you have any idea who attacked you?"

"Not yet. Look if you don't mind, Jason, I'd like to run by Lianne's room to see how she's doing."

"I don't think so," but before I could protest he smiled. "You'd better walk not run," he said and closed door.

The man is exasperating, I thought, jumping out of bed. I grabbed my clothes from the wardrobe against the wall and ducked into the bathroom.

It's not easy to dress with a sore arm and shoulder. Never mind that the trip to the hospital was unplanned and you only have the clothes you were wearing then. I pulled up my Levi's without panties, which felt gross, but my bra didn't look too bad. It would have to do and I put it on.

I'd brushed my teeth earlier with a toothbrush provided by a nurse's aide and a quick scrounging in my backpack yielded a lipstick and a comb. My panties went in a plastic bag I found in the bottom of the wastebasket and then into my purse. I was as ready as I would ever be.

I opened the door and saw a nurse's aide coming down the hall with a wheelchair. Jason Foxx motioned to her.

"No way, I'm not riding in that," I said.

"Yes, you are," said Jason. "It's hospital rules." He flapped a hand in the direction of the wheelchair.

"I don't give a big rat's behind. I'm not getting into a wheelchair." I walked past him, the aide and her wheelchair, and down to the nurse's station. I overheard voices behind me but didn't turn around.

"We ready to leave?" asked the nurse on duty using that stupid plural "we."

"Sorry, but yes," I told her. "Your hotel leaves a lot to be desired."

"Well, we're all set. Doctor wants us to take these," the nurse handed over two pill bottles. "One is for pain, and one is a muscle relaxer. Follow the directions on this sheet."

I glanced at the paper. Besides instructions on medications, the doctor noted for me to call later today for a follow-up appointment. A little soreness would be my major problem and doctors only wish to add to their coffers. I stuffed the paper into my backpack.

"Ms. Barrow, we need to make a stop by the business office to check-out first," the nurse said. "I'll call for a chair."

"I already have one," I said, glancing back to Foxx and the nurse's aide, who were standing and talking. The nurse also looked their way and while she was distracted, I walked fast towards the elevators in the opposite direction. I stepped inside and pushed 5, the floor for Lianne's room. As the doors closed I saw Jason Foxx. He and the wheelchair he pushed moved along at a good clip but not quite fast enough. I grinned at my maneuver.

Sergeant Harry Albright stood next to Lianne's bed with a bouquet of spring flowers in his hands and Kyle Raines sat in the visitor's chair next to the bed.

My first thoughts on seeing her were of when Byron was shot, except he had been in ICU with about a million tubes running everywhere. I pushed aside those memories and made myself think about the morning after I shot Garcia when Lianne came in and talked about how terrible I looked.

"You look pretty awful."

Harry stared at me. "What are *you* doing out of bed?"

He moved back so I could get closer. Lianne's eyes were closed, but she opened them at the sound of my voice.

"Insulting me, with me here flat on my back," Lianne said.

"She looks great to me," said Kyle.

"Nothing a little make-up couldn't cure," I said. I'd honestly never seen her like this—with matted hair and bare face. A shaved area with a small bandage above her right ear gleamed white.

"When my head stops whirling I'll see what I can do," Lianne said.

"Just trying to be helpful. I'm on my way home," I said. "I don't like hospitals." I had hoped to ask her if she remembered anything from Tami's trick book, but I could tell that was out of the question right now. She was obviously in no condition to answer questions.

"Can't say I blame you," Harry said.

Lianne smiled, but it was forced. "I'm not too crazy about them myself."

"Looks like you've settled in here for a time."

This time her smile was genuine. "I have the absolute worst headache. What did that guy hit me with? A Mack truck?"

"A blackjack. Are you okay besides the headache?"

"I think so. They're going to do a C.A.T. scan later today. There's a possibility of a fracture up there," Lianne said.

"Holy cow," I said. "Anything I can do?"

"Bring me a pizza later tonight." She tried to laugh and her eyes looked like they were crossing. "My head hurts so much I can't think straight. Wish I could go to sleep."

"Can't they give you something?" I asked.

"Not now. Because of the head injury," said Kyle.

"You a trauma expert now, Kyle?" I asked, keeping my tone light. My shock at him being here and ensconced as Lianne's pal or close friend had turned to curiosity.

"No," he said. "But after I got here and found her nearly out of her head with pain I called the doctor." His concern was obvious and he pressed against her hand.

Something new here? I'd never heard him use a warm and tender tone. This was not the usual Kyle come-on, I thought. Uh-oh.

"Excuse me, folks." Jason Foxx stuck his head in the door. "Zoe, you ready to go?"

"In a minute, Jason," I said and immediately realized Lianne and Harry didn't know him. I motioned him inside, introduced him and Kyle said Jason was a private investigator who we had recommended to a friend of mine.

"I'd better go, Lianne. Mr. Foxx offered to drive me home and I don't want to delay him. I'll be back. You'll probably feel more like talking later."

Her eyes were closed, but she smiled and waved one finger of good-bye.

Jason Foxx walked out first, and I told Harry and Kyle I'd see them later.

Kyle nodded and reached for Lianne's hand.

Harry Albright walked over and held out the flowers he'd been holding. I noticed a similar bouquet already in a vase on Lianne's nightstand. "I almost forgot," he said. "I brought these to you. I was coming up after leaving here."

"Harry. How sweet. Thank you."

"I'll walk out with you; we need to talk," he said.

Jason Foxx insisted I sit in the wheelchair he brought from

the third floor. I sat and he pushed. I knew from Albright's expression he'd wanted to talk to me alone, but what I could do?

As we rounded the corner from Lianne's room, a familiar voice suddenly shrieked, "Why didn't you call me, Zoe?"

My mother strode up and blocked the wheelchair.

"Mom, it's nothing," I said. "Besides, I didn't want to worry you. I know you're still worn-out from your travels."

"Not worry?" she said, her voice raised a notch. "You get assaulted, sent to the hospital, the whole thing splashed all over the newspaper and you think I might not worry?" She ended it all in a crescendo.

"Mom, I'm sorry." I looked to Jason and Harry for help. They both stared at Helene Taylor open-mouthed. She can be formidable without even trying.

Since my dad and brother are over six feet and I'm only two inches below six feet, my mother, standing four-feet-and-eleven inches and weighing in at ninety-six pounds learned to stand up to all of us. And to take us down a notch or two whenever she puts her mind to it. She looks and sounds like a much larger woman.

She's also the great goddess of social organization. She introduced herself to Jason and Harry, then dismissed them with a wave of her hand. She grabbed the wheelchair and started towards the elevator. "I've checked you out. You're free to go. You're going home with me. I've made a nice pot of vegetable soup and—"

I stopped the chair with both my feet and jumped out. "Mother, I'm not going to your house. You can take me to my place but—"

"And just why not, Missy?"

"It's not necessary. I'm fine and I want to go to my own home."

"But who'll take care of you?"

"I only have a few bruises and I can manage. I don't need a nurse."

"You also got into a gun battle the other night and you didn't bother to tell me about that either. You could have been killed."

That's when I heard it in her voice. She was scared. No wonder she was snippy. "But I didn't, because I'm a good cop and you know it." I honestly didn't know how to handle her fears and think I totally panicked. I planted a kiss on her cheek and handed her Harry's bouquet. "I'm fine, Mom, just fine. I'll call you later."

"Zoe, get in this wheelchair this instant and—"

I stopped. "Mother, I will not be treated like a six-year-old." I noticed the stairway EXIT sign, pushed open the door and walked into the stairwell. As the door closed I could hear Harry, Jason and my mother all talking at once but I couldn't understand a word.

I took the stairs quickly and when I reached ground level, took the side entrance facing the medical and professional building. Mother would go to the front lobby first. Once I got to the professional building I'll be fine, I thought. An argument with my mother isn't fun but sometimes she pushed me to the wall.

Inside the professional building, I hurried to the back entrance, sat on a bench outside and relaxed. Less than a minute later a taxi pulled up to let someone out. I waved at the driver and got in. I gave him my address, but before the taxi could pull away, Harry Albright opened the door and slid in beside me.

"Take off," he told the driver and began to laugh. "Hey, good moves, Zoe."

I had to laugh, too, as the taxi bumped out of the parking

keep my tall frame going, I tell myself, but then I starve for the next two days when I indulge.

"Want to play on my team, Lianne?" Albright asked as we got on the elevator and rode down to the second floor. The Star's night manager had offered the use one of the small meeting rooms for a command post and interrogation room.

"No can do, Harry," Lianne said. "Vice's got me on something big I can't neglect, but I can put in a few hours tonight. Zoe's available. And she's just what you need. She's good."

"Mrs. Barrow? Isn't she on desk duty?"

"Only until Monday, I'm told."

Albright still hesitated but after a moment or two he grinned. "I'll mention it to Ham, Mrs. Barrow. If you're sure you want in. Ham and I are old deer-hunting buddies. I can threaten to keep him off my deer lease if he squawks," Albright said.

I couldn't get an accurate read on him but if he wanted to give me half a chance, I damn sure would take it. I smiled, "That ought to do it. Ham's got to have his venison. And yes, I'm sure I want to be on the team. Tami was my snitch. But one request sir; please call me Zoe."

"Okay, Zoe. Now does Miss Smuts have any family?" he asked.

"None that I know about, but I can check. Her real name is Tami Louise Smith."

We got off the elevator and walked into the Nova, a room around twenty feet wide and twenty feet long. Three or four tables had been pushed together and covered with a white tablecloth and placed in the center of the room, in lieu of a conference table, and a half-dozen chairs sat around the tables. "The hotel offered this space for us to use," said Harry.

He continued. "I'll call Ham first thing tomorrow. But if

area, took a right and headed for the Mo-Pac Freeway.

"How did you know where I'd be?"

"Lucky guess. When we got to the main entrance of Seton and I saw you weren't anywhere around, I figured you'd cut across to this building."

"What happened to Mother and Jason Foxx?" I asked.

"The last I saw he and your mother were on their way to the back lobby, still arguing about checking the ladies room or the gift shop or the cafeteria."

I laughed again. "Why do I feel like a kid playing hooky?"

"Kinda fun, isn't it?" Harry's lips had a faint smile. "If I had a barracuda for a mother, I'd be intimidated too."

"Honestly, she's a sweet lady," I said. "She just gets carried away when things upset her plans. And whenever she tries to corral me, I rebel. Always have and probably always will."

We were silent for a few minutes. I was thinking about the ballroom dance lessons she signed me up for. I must have been about seven and hated to dance. Well, actually I liked to dance, what I hated was the phony genteel southern manners the teacher tried to instill because I wanted to be out playing cowboys and Indians, or cops and robbers, with my brother. It got so bad I would hide every Thursday. Sometimes mother would find me and sometimes she wouldn't. She kept making me go until my father finally said, "Enough." He was tired of paying for lessons for someone who couldn't or wouldn't learn.

My brother Chip, had it made. Anything he ever did was A-okay with Helene and Herbert Taylor. We were the perfect big-sister-toes-the-line, little-brother-gets-away-with-murder family.

Fortunately, my brother turned into a tolerable, even likable adult, and he took my side when I decided to become a police officer. It was three days before Helene would speak to either of us.

The taxi exited the freeway and only a few blocks from my apartment before I spoke again. "You wanted to talk, Harry?"

"Later," he said and nodded in the direction of the driver.

Once we got to my place, I told Harry to make himself at home, and excused myself. I found the cats asleep on my bed. They ignored me. Probably tired from worrying all night because I didn't come home, or mad at me. Most likely they were mad. "But I called Marcy this morning early to come feed you, how come you're mad?" They didn't even twitch a whisker.

I stripped and jumped into the shower. Dressed in clean underwear, a pair of clean sweats and barefoot, I joined my guest outside on the deck. He sat on the deck with his feet dangling over the edge, contemplating the lake.

Sunshine, wispy high clouds and a soft breeze hinted at an early spring. I breathed in the fresh air, expelling the anti-septic, disinfectant hospital odors that still lurked in my lungs.

"Nice place," Harry said, without turning. "Great view. You forget how pretty Town Lake and that pink granite capitol building are when you're so caught up in murder and mayhem."

"I know. Would you like coffee? Or a cold drink?"

"I'm fine," he said.

I sat down in a chaise-lounge-style deck chair and waited.

In a minute or two Harry got up and sat near my feet. "When I joined the force twenty-four years ago, women weren't in the picture. Oh, we had one or two but they were used in undercover vice operations or as meter maids."

"You don't like women police officers?"

"Well, I, uh, never had thought them effective enough on

patrol. Too many times they'd have to have a man back them up, like when they had to drag a huge guy out of an automobile."

I knew women in the department who could take on any size suspect, male or female, in any vehicle. Young cadets were well trained in martial arts and used finesse instead of muscle. I swallowed back my smart-aleck remarks. "That argument won't wash, Harry. Not in the nineties."

"Well, I've eaten my words a time or two. And I've learned women can negotiate better than men. They'll talk someone into giving up instead of resisting." He frowned. "In recent years I've had to eat crow because a woman investigator did a much better job solving a crime than a man. They're more patient and use intuition more, I think. There's some I'd stack up against any male in intelligence and competence."

I could tell he'd given the idea a lot of thought and wondered if Lianne had been instrumental in his enlightenment. "Lianne?"

"She's one of the best. No doubt about it. I've learned to look at things from an entirely different angle working with her. But I'll have to confess deep in my gut, I still think like a chauvinist a great deal of the time."

"You've made some progress if you can see that in yourself." His words sounded a whole lot like something Lianne would say.

He rubbed his eyes and yawned.

"Did you get any sleep, Harry?"

" 'Bout seventy-five minutes, right before I came up to the hospital." He yawned again. "Maybe I'll take some of that coffee you offered earlier."

Harry followed me inside, and while I made coffee, he continued.

"Zoe, what I'm trying to say . . . and I know I'm saying it

badly, is I hope you'll forgive me if I get bent out of shape sometimes. I hope you'll continue working with me, despite my occasional lapses of piggy behavior."

"You haven't shown me your bad side yet, Harry." God, the man was a dinosaur. This must be what Lianne meant when she warned me about him. However, he'd managed to get me to like him despite his admission. "Our main priority cop-to-cop has nothing to do with gender. We want to catch Tami's killer. In that, you and I have everything in common." I poured the fresh coffee and we took it back outside.

My telephone rang, but I let the answering machine pickup. It was my mother calling to apologize for trying to "mother" me and to invite me to dinner. I'd call her later. I didn't feel up to dealing with her right now.

Harry waited until we were seated at my picnic table to ask, "So somebody wanted Tami's trick book?"

"Has to be the killer. Who else knew she was dead? Who else knew the police would come looking for that book?"

"Did you see any names? We need to know."

"Lianne showed it to me. I remember a judge and a prominent businessman's name and a man's name in large red letters. Auvy, I think it said. That's about all. Lianne may remember."

"And she might not. Head traumas can scramble your brain for a few days, even a mild concussion."

"She'll probably do better when she's not in so much pain."

He yawned again. "How well do you know this Foxx guy?"

"I only met him last night. Why?"

"I found out this morning he was asking questions about Tami around the hotel last night while we were talking to the witnesses."

"You're kidding," I said. "Nothing about that should

make you suspicious. What else?"

"A female witness from the hotel came forward this morning. Says she saw a man fitting Foxx's description hanging around Room 1037 about the time Tami was killed."

"The description fit?"

"Close enough. Approximately six- six-one. One-eighty to one-ninety pounds. Said the man had on a knit cap, but she thought he had reddish hair. She wasn't real sure about the hair color though."

"Fits a lot of men," I said.

Harry sighed.

"Okay," I said. "It fits Jason Foxx too. I'm not defending him, but that description also loosely fits Richard Hebron. And Kyle Raines from my office is about that size, except he has dark hair and a beard."

"Okay, the witness could have seen the security chief or even someone entirely innocent."

"Right," I agreed.

"Hebron's a little hinky somehow and I don't like hinky. However, he's Navy, Shore Patrol, and with the Travis County Sheriff's department until a few months ago."

"Got caught up in the clean sweep when his boss lost the election, huh?"

"All the info hasn't come in from the military yet, and I still want to check out the drug dealing kick-back angle on him."

I thought about Hebron. "I don't know why," I said. "But I get the creeps when he looks at me."

A smug smile cross his lips and he said, "Intuition?"

When I said maybe, he asked, "What does your intuition tell you about Foxx?"

"He's a brash, know-it-all flirt. He says he's an ex-Houston cop." I thought about the sequence of last night's events. "Do we know the medical examiner's estimate on Tami's time of death?"

"Officer Raines says he saw Tami alive and well and in her car a few minutes after eleven, and the body was discovered at twelve-thirty, so it's a pretty safe bet for that ninety-minute time span. Doubt we'll get much closer than that."

"Foxx was at my place when I got home around midnight. I don't know what time he actually showed."

"You don't live more than five minutes from the Star. That's plenty of time."

"What's his motive?"

"Don't worry I'll find one if he's involved. I am going to check him out, just like I'll check all of them out." Harry got up, stepped over the rail and started walking.

"Hebron and Raines, too?"

Harry kept walking, but his voice floated back, "Especially those three, cause everybody's a suspect in my book."

That afternoon I made the short drive out to Pecan Groves Nursing Home, parked and went to Byron's room. "Hey, Babe," I said. "How's my guy?" I pulled a chair up beside his bed. He lay facing this way and I could pretend for a few brief minutes that we were having a nice conversation.

Before his accident, Byron knew about Tami being my snitch. We'd discussed her usefulness several times. Someone who is not in law enforcement can never totally understand police work. Good people don't want to know about the real scumbags who are out there in their city. So you soon find all your friends are cops—all your time is spent with cops. Cops marry cops. No one else understands the long hours or the loneliness. With another cop you can discuss aspects of your case and receive immediate understanding. That's one big plus of marrying a cop. I try not to think of all the minuses.

I wanted so badly to climb in beside him and talk things over. He was a good listener and often helped clarify my thoughts. I didn't do that but I did talk. Told him how vulnerable Tami had been and how someone took advantage of that fact.

I told him about her sad little room and how she'd made the best of it. "Byron, she didn't deserve to die like that."

My husband's expression didn't change even when I told him about Lianne. She had been one of his favorite people. "But don't you worry none because we both will be fine. You know my mom does all the necessary worrying in our family."

"Oh, there's this homicide cop I'm working with, name's Harry Albright. Did you ever meet him? He's one of those tough older guys—smart but still stuck in the fifties or sixties. Not too thrilled to be working with female officers. Lianne's been trying to raise his consciousness. Basically he's a decent sort, I think."

I stretched and felt the stiffness settling into my arm and shoulder. It was getting late and I felt like heading home and going straight to bed, but I'd promised Lianne I'd come by the hospital and bring her a pizza for supper.

I smoothed the sheet over Byron's shoulder. "We'll find out who killed her. All we need is a lucky break."

Byron gave me no sign that he heard as I bent over to kiss him good-bye.

The only answers and lucky breaks would come from hard investigative work and Harry Albright's determination to suspect everyone.

Deep down I knew he was right.

Immediately following the Civil War, seven officers, five white and two black, received pay checks of $65.00 a month. That amount remained in effect until 1907. In May 1882 the *Austin Daily Statesman* proclaimed that seven policemen were not enough. (Compiled from: the Austin History Center Records.)

Chapter 10

Harry Albright's remarks about Jason Foxx made me think. I didn't care much for Foxx, but to accuse him? As far as I knew he didn't know Tami and had no motive to kill her. Harry's suggestion made a point, however, to not take Mr. Foxx lightly.

Hebron, the hotel security chief, definitely knew more than he admitted. If he closed one eye to drug deals going on at the hotel and if Tami saw something she wasn't supposed to, she could have been in danger. Maybe her death had nothing to do with some berserko john she'd argued with and everything to do with dealing drugs. It made more sense that way.

Maybe the witness who mentioned the red-haired man saw Hebron. As security chief he had reason to be anywhere in the hotel. The vague description the woman gave Albright could easily fit a quarter of Austin's male population. I knew Albright would check Foxx and Hebron down to what brand of underwear they wore and that he'd find out if either one had something to hide.

I had done a few stretching exercises to work the stiffness out of my right shoulder and arm and played with the cats after Harry left. My trip to the hospital had left me sleep-deprived but I managed a nap. Another hot shower and three ibuprofen later my arm and shoulder felt almost back to normal while my skin looked as wrinkled as an un-ironed cotton blouse.

The warm spring-like day drew to a close and mindful of the drop in the temperature when the sun went down, I dressed in a white-and-gold cable knit sweater, a pair of black

hate the fish and she hates the peppers.

Seton offers valet parking to visitors. Just drive up the two-lane curved drive to the hospital's front door and let a valet-person park your car, exactly like you'd do at a swanky restaurant or hotel. For those of us who can't afford valets and whose legs must continue to do the walking, they also offer self-parking on the east edge of the front grounds.

A triangle-shaped garden between the curved front drive and the two-way regular drive led to the self-parking area and to the city street. Plants and trees decorate the drives and next to the front door is a statue of Elizabeth Ann Seton, American's first native-born saint for whom the hospital is named. A bucolic setting which contrasted the pain and suffering inside.

Avery Peppard was visible in the front lobby as I neared the glass entry doors; pacing but I almost didn't recognize him. This was not the man I'd met for dinner a short time ago. He hadn't shaved in days and his clothing looked as rumpled as if it had just come out of a cold dryer. He had a black felt hat pulled down low and wore sunglasses.

"Thank God you came," he said. A fine sheen of sweat shone on his forehead.

"What on earth has happened?"

"Zoe, you're going to think I'm crazy." He hit his forehead with the heel of his hand and kept hitting himself four or five times. He looked just like the guy on the TV commercial who forgot about drinking the sponsor's juice.

"I won't think you're nuts, just spit it out."

"They tried to kill me." He walked a few steps away and turned his back.

I glanced around. I took Peppard's arm gently and led him over to a corner and made him sit on a sofa beside me.

The lobby was half-full, people sitting, some milling

around. Most were obviously visitors but others were patients in robes and slippers with plastic bracelets on their wrists. This wasn't like a waiting room worry or deathwatch—cheerfulness permeated the air in this lobby. These folks were getting well; many probably going home tomorrow. No one paid any special attention to us.

"Who tried to kill you?"

"Mary Anna Margaret, I guess. Or her hit man." He held out shaky hands; the nails chewed to the quick on at least four fingers. He then made fists, letting them rest on his knees. "A man attacked me. This guy wore a navy long coat and a navy knit cap. He bumped into me outside my office and I think I saw a knife in his hand."

"Did he try to stab you or make a threatening gesture towards you?"

"No. He just bumped me and kept on going. I think he was trying to show me how easy it is to get at me."

The story just didn't make much of a case for attempted murder. Oh I believed someone, an unsavory looking someone, may have bumped into Peppard. The part I doubted was the knife. In his current state of mind, I thought Peppard could easily have imagined the whole thing. Maybe this guy held a ballpoint pen or some innocent object. "This happened outside your office?"

He nodded.

"When?"

"About three o'clock today. I decided to leave early and go home. I'm not sleeping much." He leaned his head back and rubbed his eyes with both fists.

"For a little while after it happened, I was okay. I got to my car and decided I didn't really want to go home. I just started driving. I drove north out Interstate 35, came back and drove out to Lake Travis. But the more I thought about it, the more scared I got. That's when I called you."

I could see this was going to take time. I didn't know how, but I had to convince him this had all been a big mistake. Several questions came to mind immediately but Lianne's pizza was getting cold. I honestly didn't believe he had been in danger, yet I didn't want to seem unconcerned. And why me and not Jason Foxx?

"Avery," I indicated the pizza box, "let me take this upstairs to my friend. You sit here and relax. When I get back we'll work this thing out, I promise." He leaned his head back and closed his eyes. "That's right, you're safe here, take a little nap if you can."

I took the elevator to Lianne's room. Naturally she looked great. Freshly combed hair and light but effective make-up applied. She wore a forest green velour robe that set off her auburn hair to perfection and when her complaints started I could tell she felt better.

"Dang it, Zoe. I want to go home. But they won't let me. It's just stupid."

"What did the doctor say?"

She shrugged. "Not until tomorrow, he said. But I feel fine."

"If there's a small fracture . . ."

"The CAT scan didn't show anything."

"Good, but if the doctor lets you go now and you got into trouble . . ."

"I know," she smiled. "The doctor said I might have a bleeder in my brain or something. But if I did then I could sue his ass off for malpractice."

"Might not be worth it. You might be dead."

"Why are you always right?"

"I'm not always," I said, "but this time I am." She grinned.

"See if you feel up to helping me out. I'm wondering if you remember anything from Tami's book."

Lianne closed her eyes and wrinkled her forehead. "I remember a car dealer—you know the one who does all those loud commercials. I can see his face but can't call his name."

"Larry Bob Mayhan?"

"Yeah. That's him."

"I don't remember him. I'm sure I saw a name in red letters *Auvy*. And part of that phone number, 555."

"Sure. 555-2804."

"Great. See your brains are still in there, but you just have to let them rest."

As we talked, I'd opened the pizza and placed it on her bed tray. I took a small slice for myself and ate it.

"So do you have plans? Wanna keep me company? I'm bored silly."

"I can't. I've got this minor crisis involving a friend of Levi's. The man is downstairs waiting in the lobby to talk to me."

I found a Dixie cup in the bathroom and drank some water.

"That's okay. Kyle will be here in a few minutes." She gave me a look I couldn't read.

Our assault last night needed some questions answered and I'd hoped come back up later. I'd rather not intrude on their time. "You know he's married." I made it a statement, not a question.

"I know. Just don't say anything. He's being a good friend which I need right now."

"Right." I leaned over and gave her a hug. "I'll probably see you tomorrow."

Peppard sat right where I'd left him, head back, eyes closed. I thought he was asleep, but when I sat beside him on the sofa, he opened his eyes.

"They've bugged my office," he said, "and probably my car and telephone."

"Why do you think that?"

"Because they know every move I make." He looked at his hands and picked at a torn cuticle. "Why don't you get your investigator, uh, Jason Foxx to sweep for—"

"I don't I trust him."

I sighed. Totally paranoid. The man has lost it. But I couldn't help wondering where Foxx was when all this happened. If he'd been on the job maybe Peppard wouldn't have gotten so upset. "Avery, I've spoken to Foxx. This man is an ex-cop from Houston. He seems competent to me." Peppard didn't need to learn of my suspicions about Foxx. No use upsetting him any more than he already was right now.

"But M.M.'s boyfriend is a cop or an ex-cop," he said. "Maybe her lover is Foxx. I just know someone follows me every minute of the day. It's unnerving." He crossed and uncrossed his legs and avoided looking at me. "They're out to kill me and they're going to get away with it."

"Avery, Jason Foxx is new to this area so I hardly think he's your wife's lover." He didn't comment so I continued. "And I know for a fact Jason is watching you, following you. That's the only way he can discover this guy's identity—follow you—see who's paying special attention to you."

"All I know is that when someone flashes a knife, I know I'm in deep hockey." He wasn't trying to be funny either.

I could tell he wasn't reassured. "Okay. Let's go over it again. Tell me exactly what happened from the time you left your office at three o'clock."

He repeated the whole incident, and although I questioned him closely I didn't get much more in the way of details. What he told me just didn't add up to an attack in my book. If his wife's lover was going to kill him, why flash a knife? Why put Peppard on guard? Seems to me like a killer would kill and get it over with period.

The way Peppard looked and acted was a puzzler too. This was not the self-assured man I'd met for dinner a few days ago. Not this quivering bundle of nerves sitting beside me chewing his nails.

I didn't want to be rude but . . . "Avery, what's happened to you?"

"What's happened?" He looked puzzled briefly and he wouldn't look directly at me. "You mean besides someone trying to kill me?"

"I mean you look like something the cats drug up and played with for hours." This disintegration had taken place over two or three days not in just the last few hours.

"How would you feel knowing a killer is stalking you?" he asked. "Knowing that the next minute might be your last." He stuck a finger in his mouth and chewed on a fingernail and continued to avoid my eyes as he spoke. "You'd look like hell, too," he said, "if you were living in fear like I am."

Maybe I would. Everyone reacts differently to fear. But Peppard headed a multi-million dollar corporation where he had to be tough against cutthroat competition. The man was primed for toughness and his actions seemed extreme in my book.

Maybe Jason Foxx could enlighten me. I had a few questions for him, too—like what was he doing when this alleged attack happened? "I think Foxx should be in on this," I said. "Do you have a number where you can reach him?"

Peppard wasn't too happy with the idea of calling the P.I. but he gave me the number.

When I reached the investigator on his cell phone and explained what was happening, Foxx said, "Thank God. I've been searching everywhere for Peppard since three this afternoon. He had an argument with . . . Oh hell, I'm coming over there. I'll explain everything then."

"We'll wait here in the front lobby."

"Avery," I said, when I got back to him. "Foxx was watching you today and saw what happened. Did you argue with that man?"

He jumped up and began pacing again. "I just wish I felt some of your confidence."

"I think you'll feel differently after you hear what Foxx has to say." Peppard could quickly get on my nerves if he didn't calm down a little. I patted the sofa cushion beside me. "Sit down, try to relax, he'll be here soon."

He sat, but only for a minute before jumping up and pacing again. It was pointless to try and stop him.

When Foxx arrived the two men just glared at each other, then began a heated discussion, blame and guilt flew around like slinging mud. We were getting nowhere. I was starving and suggested we head to Denny's for coffee.

There's not enough leg room in my car for three people so Foxx led the way over in his van and Peppard rode with me. I felt tired and headachy from the lack of food and sleep and shushed Peppard up when he tried to talk. After that he stayed silent throughout the trip.

We found a booth in a quiet corner near the back, Peppard and I on one side and Foxx opposite. They were hungry too, so we all ordered cheeseburgers, fries and iced tea.

"Okay, Jason," I said when the waitress left with our orders, "tell me what you saw happen today."

"I was at my stake-out across from Mr. Peppard's office. You know where his office is?"

I shook my head. "Not exactly." I knew it was around Highland Mall but no other details.

"You know the backside of Highland Mall? His office is in a building across the street from the mall. A parking lot surrounds the building. It's a busy area with traffic coming and going and folks who've been to the mall driving through so it's a good place for a stake-out. No one pays much attention to a guy sitting in a van. There's a gentleman's club next door to add to traffic activity, too.

"Anyway," Foxx gestured to Peppard, "he came out about three, glanced about nervously and started along the sidewalk away from where I sat. A man came out from the far corner of the building and bumped into him. The guy looked like a bum asking for a handout to me. I saw Peppard get upset, but I had no idea why."

"You'd be upset, if you'd seen that knife." Peppard's tone was contemptuous.

"I jumped out and headed towards Mr. Peppard," said Jason. "He looked okay. I mean he was still walking around and there wasn't any blood flowing, so I took off after this guy. I followed him all the way over to the mall. The place was jammed with a lot of mid-afternoon shoppers. He ducked into the J.C. Penney store and he must have jumped on their down escalator and out into the mall area again because I lost him."

"Hah, some bodyguard you are," Peppard said, his voice growing louder. "I thought you were going to protect me; that's what I hired you for."

The waitperson interrupted with our food, just as I placed my hand on Peppard's arm to quieten him. After she left I asked Avery, "I thought you hired Mr. Foxx to find out who Mary Margaret's lover was?"

"Well, that too. But he was supposed to keep me from being killed."

"Well, nobody tried to kill you." Foxx's voice rose as he

got defensive. "So I lost the guy, so sue me."

Foxx took large bites of his burger and finished it in a matter of seconds. I wondered how he kept from getting ulcers.

Peppard ate slowly and kept his voice down as he said, "Hell, I don't want to sue you. I just want to keep from dying. Is that so unreasonable?" He asked me, "Am I being difficult?"

I shook my head and sipped my tea.

"No," said Foxx. "But I told you in the beginning it would be practically impossible to keep someone from killing you if they really wanted to. You're wearing your Kevlar vest I got you, aren't you?"

Peppard nodded.

"If someone tried to stab you, the knife could penetrate that but chances are he won't try again that close. And you have a certain amount of protection from a bullet," I said. "There's not much else that can be done." Peppard might be my father-in-law's good pal and I wanted to stay in Levi's good graces, but I'd just about had it with both these guys.

"But I'm paying you good money to keep me alive." Peppard voice took on the contemptuous tone again.

"The Kevlar vest I bought for Peppard will even withstand a knifing," Jason said. "It's the latest technology and Peppard was willing to pay so I got him the best."

"Didn't know they had such a thing," I said. "But it sounds as if Mr. Foxx has covered all bases."

"Not if someone is stalking me and trying to kill me." Peppard's face got red. "And I hate wearing this stupid vest; it's hot and bulky and heavy."

"So take it off, I don't care," said Foxx.

Both men's voices were getting louder again as each tried to make his point. "We'll never get anywhere if you guys keep arguing," I said. "Both of you back off and—"

Jason Foxx's beeper went off and he excused himself to make a phone call. While he was gone, I told Avery to lighten up. He calmed down and finished his food.

Foxx slid back into the booth and Peppard started firing questions at him. What had he done about finding the man who'd tried to stab him? What had he done to identify Mary Margaret's lover? Each question was asked and answered without regard to nicety. Their belligerence kept increasing.

"That's it," I said. "I'm outta here. You two thrash it out and you," I pointed to Jason Foxx, "call me tomorrow because I have some questions for you." I scooted against Peppard forcing him to get up to let me out.

Peppard said, "I rode over here with you."

"Jason can drive you to wherever you want to go."

"But—"

"Look," I said to Peppard. "It would take an army of cops to do what you're expecting one man to do. I still think he can help you if you'll let him but I'm exhausted and this bickering will get you nowhere. Tomorrow when you've both chilled a little, maybe I can find out what actually happened today, but I've had it for tonight." I placed a five-dollar bill and two ones down for my food, turned, and walked away.

In 1880, William Henry Porter (a.k.a. O. Henry) complained once about the cocaine fiends who gathered at night on Seventh Street and Porter wasn't the sort of guy who ruffled easily. But not until 1898, was a city ordinance passed banning the sale and use of cocaine. A string of busts were made in Guytown after a month long investigation by APD. (Compiled from: Austin History Center Records: *Austin American Statesman Monthly Almanac* articles.)

Chapter 11

The next morning after a brisk shower and two cups of coffee I jotted down all my recollections from Tami's book. I'd tried to make some sense of it last night but my brain had rebelled and gone blank.

A short time later, Ham Hamilton called to say he'd assigned me to Harry Albright. "Officially you're still on administrative duty, but I can ease you back for this. Since you knew Tami Smuts I hesitated," he said. "But I've never won an argument with Harry in my life; he's too good at arm twisting."

Ham was silent then, presumably recalling some past incident where he'd argued with Harry and lost. When he spoke again, he said, "You're familiar with the players. Should make things easier and, talk about good experience—might even help your career on down the road."

"I'll try to keep my personal feelings out of it."

"I wouldn't have agreed otherwise," he told me. "I should warn you though, Harry will hang on this one until there's nothing more—"

Someone started banging against my front door, the noise sounding so much like a jackhammer, I couldn't hear him. "Just a minute, Ham. Someone's at my door."

"That'll be Harry," said Ham, and I laid the receiver down.

Sure enough Harry's face showed through the distortion of the peephole when I looked. I unlocked it. "Come on in, I'm talking to Ham." Harry held out a box from Krispy Kreme.

"Tell Ham good-bye," Harry said, "and let's rock and roll. The bottom-feeders are all sleeping this time of day and that's when I like to pound on doors. It shakes them up."

I picked up my receiver and told Hamilton he was right about my early visitor and thanked him. "Don't forget where you belong, Zoe. I don't want to lose you to Homicide. At least not yet—you're one of the best players in this unit." I promised to keep him up to date and replaced the phone.

While Harry drank some coffee and started in on the doughnuts, I dressed in a red and black plaid turtleneck sweater, red slacks and my sneakers.

When I walked into the kitchen, Harry held out the travel mug he'd found on my counter and filled it with coffee. "I don't know how you take this."

"A little milk and sugar," I said, and fixed it that way.

"Should have known you're one of those debutantes that doctor it up. Any other delaying tactic you can think of? Need to go to the potty?"

I grabbed the coffee out of his outstretched hand, picked up the box with the three doughnuts he'd left and headed out the front door. "Anyone ever tell you what a pain in the ass you are?"

"My ex-wife used that exact expression daily the last six months we were married," Harry said.

"Smart woman," I muttered under my breath, hoping he'd heard me. If he did, he kept his retorts to himself.

We took his car and he burned rubber all the way to the corner. I'd figured Harry to be a Sunday-afternoon-type driver but noooo. He drove like a maniac at Daytona. I was glad for a seatbelt and the coffee mug with a lid. Don't get me wrong, he was good, constantly aware of each car on the road, but he liked speed.

We reached the interstate and squealed around the corner

to the entrance ramp, heading north. Town Lake looked calm and placid as we crossed it and even at this early hour joggers were out making their way along the lake edges. The pink granite capitol building gleamed bright in the early morning sun as we blew past downtown and continued north. "Who're we going to see?" I asked.

"A man named Stevie Crooks."

"A small time hood and sometimes pimp. Probably seen me with Tami but he doesn't know I'm a cop."

"Is it a problem?"

"Possibly."

"I'd better talk to him alone then."

When we reached Manor Road, he exited and went east. This was another spring-like day and the sky was that glorious shade of clear blue that you sometimes see on those picture postcards from vacationing friends writing to say "glad you aren't here." Made me happy to be living in central Texas instead of somewhere up north where it was still snowing and five degrees above zero.

"Harry, I've got a scenario we could play with Stevie."

He spotted a STOP-n-GO market, pulled in, and screeched to a halt. Cutting the engine, he turned to me and said, "Let's hear it."

I hesitated and took a bite of my jelly doughnut. It wasn't easy to eat while Harry was driving.

"Just spit it out, Zoe. The plan, not the doughnut."

"What if I act like you have me in custody and—"

"Can I handcuff you?"

I cut my eyes up at him and said, "Yeah. Right, Harry."

"Just thought I'd ask." He smiled. "We'll keep it simple. You stay here and I'll go roust Stevie-boy."

"But I know enough to get an accurate read on him." He was shaking his head before I could finish. "It's—"

"You might have to use him next week or next month in Ham's unit and if we blow your cover—"

I could see the logic. And since my team was about to get a line on those Jamaicans they'd been watching since that night at the Texas Star, I couldn't argue. Except I hated it.

"Okay." I opened the door and got out. Harry laid down a stripe of black leaving the parking lot. "Hotrod Harry," I muttered.

I exchanged two dollar bills for quarters and dimes and went outside to the pay phone. I fed the box thirty-five cents and punched out 555-2804. Again there was no answer. An office with nine to five workers. I'd try again later.

Another fifty cents of my change bought today's *Austin American Statesman*. I spread the paper out atop a large trashcan outside, opened up to the funnies, sipped my coffee and ate the other doughnut. This one was chocolate-covered. I'm a chocoholic but never did care much for it on doughnuts. Krispy Kreme changed my mind; it was delicious.

"Blondie" was so-so, "Cathy" was a grinner, and I got a chuckle out of "Garfield." Saddest thing to realize Snoopy and Charlie Brown were not new but the reruns still gave me a pick-up each morning.

I finished the comics and turned to the Lifestyle for Ann Landers's column. The first letter was from a woman who'd spent seven years in an affair with a married man and wanted to know if Ann thought the man was leading her on. Couldn't help thinking about Lianne and Kyle Raines making goo-goo eyes at each other in her hospital room. I didn't think they were actually going out—yet. At least, I hoped not. I'd bet money Kyle's the type to stay with his little wife.

Traffic in and out of the gas-station-cum-small-market was heavy. Cars with hard-working folks who needed gasoline, cigarettes, or coffee and pastry made up the bulk of the stoppers. I people-watched while scanning the news and sports. Construction workers, a mailman, several secretaries and two junior executive types hurriedly made their stops and went away. A young woman and a little girl, who looked to be about three, sitting beside her pulled into the parking space in front of me, got out and went inside. The woman was eight-and-a-half months pregnant and left her child in the car.

Stupid woman. How did she know I wasn't a car thief or child molester? I debated about arresting her for endangerment to a minor, but she was in and out in under two minutes. I kept my distance and my mouth shut. An extra hour of paperwork wasn't worth the hassle. Okay so I'm sucker for pregnant women.

A black Toyota pick-up truck with those oversized tires on it cruised by twice. The Mexican-American male driver drove at a normal speed but slowed to a crawl when directly in front. Probably casing the place, I thought. Cop mentality on overtime, Zoe? Man is either looking for an address or looking to score. Either way why work myself up?

When enough time had passed to get bored out of my skull, Harry came back.

"Stevie claims to know nothing from nothing," said Harry as I slid in beside him.

"That figures."

"He swears Tami left Room 1204 at eleven and that's the last he saw of her. She told him she was going home and he believed her." We sat in front of the store while he filled me in on the rest of his talk with Stevie.

"You think he's telling the truth?"

"Mostly. He's holding something back, but whether it involves Tami or his high-roller's meeting is anyone's guess."

"How did you explain knowing he was at the hotel that night?"

"I told him an off-duty cop had spotted him and Tami there at about eight-thirty and saw them going into room 1204," said Harry. "Strangely enough he didn't question it, but he wouldn't elaborate on why they were there or who they were visiting."

"So Stevie wasn't all that useful."

"Well, I think we can eliminate him from the suspect list for now. I do like to get all my ducks in a row."

"Did you get anything on the person who rented room 1204?" I asked.

"According to hotel records, Stevie reserved the suite and paid cash for it."

"For a business meeting?"

"Of course," said Harry. "For persons unknown and for some unnamed business. Stevie's not about to talk about who these folks were. There's no way I can force it out of him short of using a rubber hose. Ahhhh, how I long for the good old days."

"Too bad we lost that trick book," I said. "Our snatch-and-grabber must have been her killer. I mean no one else knew she was dead, yet."

"Not necessarily."

Harry must be slipping a mental gear, I thought, but before I could come up with a comment, he added, "Jason Foxx and Richard Hebron knew she was dead. The college boys working security knew she was dead. With all the excitement going on Stevie and whoever he was with could have known, too. Any one of them could have stolen the book and not be the killer." He banged his hand on the steering wheel. "Any one of them could only be trying to hide the fact they were in the book. Nothing more. A married dude covering his ass."

"But of the ones we know about—Foxx is divorced, Stevie's never been married and isn't Hebron single?" Harry agreed Hebron wasn't married. "I can't see the college boys being worried, everyone knows about their raging hormones. I wouldn't be surprised if they were in her book. But okay, I'll bow to superior wisdom—our assailant doesn't have to be the murderer."

Harry turned the ignition. "Or your assailant could be the killer. For instance, let's say it was Stevie's pal. He's a big dealer who doesn't want the police looking at him too closely. Maybe he was even Tami's supplier and knew his name was in her book. He wouldn't want—"

"As far as I know Tami was off drugs, but she could have threatened to blow the whistle on him." I suddenly realized Harry was ready to back out. "Hold up a minute, Harry. I need to make a phone call before we leave." And I told him what Lianne and I remembered from Tami's book and how I'd been trying that phone number all morning. He cut the engine and settled back, picking up my newspaper.

Still no answer. I got back into the car. "Where to now?"

Harry threw the newspaper into the back seat. "What if Richard Hebron was dealing on the side and Tami found out," he said. "She might've tried a little extortion. Said she'd turn him in to the cops if he didn't pay. He's got one sweet deal as the Star's security honcho, one he wouldn't want to jeopardize."

"Makes sense," I said.

"And it moves Hebron higher up on my suspect list. We need to do what I intended to do yesterday and never got around to—have a talk with the narcs—see what they know about this guy. Any objections?"

"You're driving."

Harry raced back down the interstate and in only minutes we were parked under the freeway's overpass directly across from police headquarters. He headed to the narcotics office and I went up to my office to ask Lieutenant Hamilton about Hebron. There were so many drug-related-repeat offenders I couldn't remember them all.

"Zoe?" Kyle Raines called out as soon as I entered. "Who in the world is this Peppard guy? You've been getting phone calls from him all morning. The man is driving me crazy." He handed over four pink telephone message slips.

I walked to my desk, glancing at the slips and did a double take. In the space for name Kyle had written—Auvy Peppard. In the space for telephone number was written 555-2800.

"I'll be a monkey's grandma," I said aloud and walked back towards Kyle. "Peppard's first name is Avery—how did you come up with Auvy?"

Kyle shrugged his shoulders. "How would I know? Sounded like he said Auvy to me. A nickname maybe?"

"Thank you, Kyle, baby." I gave him a big hug while he struggled to keep from falling out of his chair. "I owe you a beer for this one."

"I know I'm swell, but what did I do?" Kyle regained his balance and tried to hug me back.

"Auvy at 555-2804. In Tami's book," I said. "I've dialed it all morning trying to find out who Auvy was. Turns out this number is Peppard's office." I stared at Kyle, thinking. "He's probably got a rotating number system: 2800, 2801, 2802, 2803, 2804. And he uses the 2804 as his private line. Gives it out to only a few people. Damn. I had a feeling I knew that number."

The Austin Superintendent of Police, concerned about traffic accidents, announced a strict enforcement against reckless driving. A reminder from the police: speed limit for automobiles or motorcycles is 16 mph on the streets and 8 mph on corners. (Compiled from: Austin History Center Records: *Austin American Statesman Monthly Almanac* articles.)

Levi's, and my black dress boots. My promise to visit Lianne tonight was at the top of my agenda.

The telephone rang. My mother? Answer or not? I flipped a mental coin, lost and picked up the receiver.

"Zoe?" Avery Peppard sounded stressed-out big time. "I need to talk to you."

"What's wrong?"

"I'm, uh, I'm too exposed at this pay phone. Could we meet? It's urgent."

"I'm on my way to Seton Hospital to visit a friend." I checked my watch. "Meet me in the lobby. Say about seven?"

"I'll look for you; you probably won't recognize me." He broke the connection abruptly.

What's going on? I wondered. Peppard acted like someone in a spy thriller. Like this business of being exposed at a pay phone? And why wouldn't I recognize him? And why me instead of his investigator? Useless speculation, I thought, and pushed Peppard out of my mind briefly.

As I drove I admired the sky. Fluffy white clouds turned pink and gold and deep indigo with the setting of the sun. One pink cloud in the eastern sky looked like a huge swirl of cotton candy. It reminded me of being eight years old and going to the circus with my dad. He'd bought me a huge bag of the pink confection and I ate so much I was sick half the night. But it had been worth it, to see the elephants and tigers and watch the trapeze artists. Dad and I giggled all the way home and in the bathroom later as I threw up and he wiped my face, I kept telling him how I wanted to run away and join the circus. He didn't laugh. He very seriously said I'd have to be at least ten years old before I could leave home alone. That's the last good time I remember with my dad.

I stopped at The Brick Oven for a large pizza with everything except anchovies and jalapenos to take to Lianne—I

Chapter 12

Avery Peppard involved with Tami Louise? The whole idea blew my mind. The businessman and the hooker? Not too uncommon if you looked at it that way.

I dialed 555-2804 again—no answer. He wasn't in his office. I tried 555-2800.

"Peppard Interests," a cheerful voice answered.

"This is Zoe Barrow returning Mr. Peppard's call."

"Oh, yes, Ms. Barrow. Mr. Peppard asked that I give you a message and to impress upon you how urgent this is," she said. Her tone changed to a conspiratorial whisper. "He wants to meet at the same place you met last night. He wouldn't even tell me where but said you'd know. He'll wait until noon. He has important information regarding your case—whatever that means." Her voice grew softer, barely discernable. "He said for you to please come alone."

"I understand." And I couldn't resist it: "Did he give you contingency plans in the event I didn't call before noon?"

"Certainly, Ms. Barrow. Shall I tell you those?"

Why was I not surprised? "No, that's fine, thank you." I placed the receiver back on the hook. God, the man's taken paranoia to the extreme.

"Have you got a car I can use?" I asked Lieutenant Hamilton. "Harry Albright drove me in this morning and I've got an errand to run."

"Where's Harry?"

"Over talking to some of his narc pals. I'll be back before he misses me." Hamilton threw me a set of car keys. "Take that Thunderbird I've been using."

133

Peppard sat in the same the corner of the hospital lobby where we'd talked last night. He looked even more rumpled, and I wondered if he'd spent the night on the lobby sofa.

"Zoe, thank God." He jumped up and grabbed my arm. "I thought you'd never get my message. We have to talk."

"Well, that's why I'm here." Peppard released me and I sat on the sofa. "And I expect you'll tell me the full story about Tami Louise Smuts?"

His face registered shock then resignation. "I've been a fool, an utter fool." He sat down.

"You knew her professionally?"

"Not well. I saw her only occasionally. I met her a year ago when I had some out-of-town clients who wanted to party. I don't remember now who recommended her." He stuck a finger to his mouth and chewed the nail.

"Strictly a business arrangement," he said, "for clients. But it worked well. I'd call, make the appointment and we'd talk. You know, about which client liked her to play a role or which one was a prude even when he was in bed. We formed an odd conspiratorial camaraderie, like old buddies setting up blind dates for friends."

I didn't interrupt, not wanting to stop his out pouring.

"One evening a couple of months ago," he said, "I ran into her at the Galaxy Room, you know the restaurant on top of the Star?"

I nodded.

"A client had stood me up and since neither she nor I had had dinner, I asked her to join me. We laughed and talked and both had too much to drink. I told her about M.M. running hot and cold in the sex department in recent weeks. Next thing I knew I'd rented a room. God, she was just what this old man needed for his ego. It never happened again except for the other night."

"You saw Tami the night she died?" He was nodding his head before I finished. No wonder Peppard was falling apart.

He continued and I didn't interrupt. "Some clients and I had dinner there and the party broke up somewhere around eleven. I saw Tami walking out the front door as I rode down the glass-sided elevator, but she didn't see me, of course.

"Just as I got outside she'd started her car engine. She turned her head to back up and spotted me and waved. I hurried over and we talked briefly. Suddenly I realized how lonely I'd been for weeks. How much I wanted her right then. I asked if she'd go back inside with me. She said she only had about two hours before her next customer. A friendly bellhop she knew gave her a room key." He buried his face in his hands and his shoulders shook.

I waited a moment and asked softly, "What happened next, Avery?"

He raised an anguished face. "I didn't kill her if that's what you think."

"Just tell me about it, Avery."

"We had sex. Afterwards, she said she had to make an important phone call so I showered first. I got dressed and gave her some money and I left."

His voice broke and his eyes swam. "Do you believe me, Zoe? She was okay when I left. I swear to you she was alive."

His story sounded straightforward, but I've heard many stories that sounded good and yet the person was lying through their teeth. Maybe I wanted to believe him because I'd felt sorry for him, especially with the situation with his wife, and I knew I lacked objectivity right now. "All right, Avery. We need to go downtown and talk to the detective in charge of the case. You can make a statement to him."

Boy, I wished now I'd waited on Harry. If I tried to call him now, it could blow this whole thing. And getting into a car with Peppard might not be the smartest move, but it looked like my only option at the moment. "And why did Tami call you 'Auvy'?"

"When Byron was little—" He stopped and looked at me. I kept my face neutral and he continued. "When your husband was little, he couldn't say Avery, it came out Auvy. The nickname sort of stuck.

"Can you imagine what I've been going through? When I heard about Tami's murder and I thought the police would find my fingerprints in that room. And I'd had sex with her. Isn't there some way to identify a man from his semen? It's driving me crazy. Not to mention how someone's stalking me, trying to kill me." He reached for my hand. "It's like I'm in some horror movie, Zoe, honest to God."

I extracted my hand slowly. "You're right, it's nightmarish, but all the more reason to talk to my partner. Harry Albright's good. He'll give you a fair shake, Avery."

"You probably know what's best. And if I get arrested at least I'll be protected from my wife's hit man."

"No one's going to arrest you. You're just going in with me to make a statement."

We began walking to the front. The main door is a revolving one that moves automatically with partitions wide enough for a wheelchair. A nurse ahead of us pushed a chair with a new mother and a baby wrapped in a pink blanket. The nurse, juggled the chair and a service cart loaded with flowers, plants, a suitcase and a diaper bag, by using one hand on each. Ten feet from the entrance an older woman stood next to a burgundy-colored Chevrolet, unlocking the passenger side door.

Congestion filled the triple-lane, curving front drive. A station wagon and yellow taxi sat behind the Chevy and on the other side of it, a second yellow cab and a blue Toyota waited—both cars held a driver and both had engines running.

The struggling nurse maneuvered the chair, but I offered to help, taking the flower cart as she accepted my offer.

Avery and I followed, walking side by side. I pushed the cart towards the burgundy car.

Without warning a popping sound exploded against my ears as it echoed and reverberated against the concrete under-hangings of the portico. I recognized the sound immediately.

The safety of mother and baby came first in my thoughts, but I was closer to Peppard. I placed my hand on his head and pushed. "Get down and stay down," I said.

I swiveled left, ducking low, clawed for and found my gun and sprinted towards the wheelchair.

The young mother stood in the open doorway of the vehicle with the baby in her arms.

"Down," I yelled to the nurse, who still had both hands on the wheelchair. "I'm a cop and that was a gunshot."

She and the mother looked petrified at seeing me with a gun in my hand, but I yanked the chair aside and shoved the frozen young woman, baby included, down across the front seat. "Get in there and stay down. I'm a police officer. Keep your head down."

A second shot rang out and the older woman, at the rear door on the driver's side, jumped inside the Chevy and sprawled across the back seat.

A high-pitched keening came from behind me. I turned and saw the nurse crawling on her belly along the walkway. Was she hit?

Somehow, above the screams that had already begun I heard a car engine being gunned—the sound coming from every direction and echoing. I peeked over the car door and saw a yellow cab, noted the number was 1041, as it made an abrupt left turn into the front driveway. The driver gunned the engine, and its tires protested the abuse as it headed for the street.

He was going too fast and I knew it was futile, but I ran across and into the triangle flower garden median. I tripped on a tree root and fell on one knee.

I heard a screech of brakes, then metal ripped and tore somewhere out near the street. I beat my fist against my leg in frustration, stood and was rewarded with a final glimpse of the driver as the cab completed its turn to the west.

I hurried back, expecting to see the nurse dead or dying. But she was on her knees beside Avery.

"Oh, my God," I said. She had to use both hands in an effort to stop the blood that pumped from his upper left torso. Avery's rumpled white shirt had turned crimson and blood puddled around him.

It happened in 1953. Investigators were looking into a wild brawl in a quiet north side neighborhood. Three shots were fired, one man was beaten with a metal pipe. Two men charged with assault-with-intent-to murder. (Excerpted from: *Austin American Statesman Monthly Almanac* articles.)

Chapter 13

Grabbing the diaper bag from the service cart, I ran to where Avery lay, sat down next to the nurse and unzipped the bag. Pulling out handfuls of Newborn Pampers, I motioned to the nurse. She was older, with salt and pepper hair, a wide nose on her narrow face and dark eyes. She radiated experience and competence. She lifted one hand and we put the disposable diapers on top of the bloody area and she continued applying pressure.

"Damn you, Avery, where's your vest? You silly so-in-so, I'll bet you took it off."

The nurse stanching the blood flow looked at me as if I was slightly nuts.

Another nurse came outside the glass entry doors. "E.R. is on the way," she said. She was young and her long blonde hair was pulled back into a ponytail. She stood at Avery's feet looking down. "Do we need to start C.P.R.?"

"Not yet," the older nurse said. "So far, he's breathing on his own."

A trauma team from the emergency room soon burst out the door and moments later they had an I.V. in Avery's arm, an oxygen mask on his face and were getting ready to place him on a gurney. I stared as they carted him away. He didn't look good, his face as white and pasty as Elmer's glue. The older nurse went inside along with the gurney, her hands rusty-red streaked and the young blonde nurse followed, her ponytail bouncing from side to side.

I wasn't sure, but probably no more than two or three minutes had passed. The medical team who worked on Avery looked like top-notch people. If he had a chance it would be due to their quickness and efforts.

I looked out at the street and walked partway down the curved drive. Only one car was banged up. The driver was talking to a knot of people who had gathered.

I returned to the burgundy Chevrolet to check on the new mother and baby. Both were crying. "Is everyone okay?" I asked.

The older woman—I assumed she was the new grand-mother—sat up in the back seat and shook her head. "Nooo, I'm not okay. I wet my pants." In her mid-forties, with dark hair that curled around her face, she was nicely dressed in a pair of light blue twill pants with a dark blue cable knit sweater. A huge wet spot was visible on her slacks. A bright pink color crept up her neck and into her face.

"Don't worry about it," I told her. "I'd have wet mine if there'd been time."

She threw back her head and laughed, then crawled out and walked around to the new mother and baby. She placed both arms around them and held them close.

I told them they needed to hang around until more cops arrived because they'd have to give a statement.

"I couldn't drive right now, even if I wanted to," the older woman said.

The words were barely out of her mouth when a police car drove up, stopping on the far side of the Chevy. An officer strode over and I pulled my badge out, holding it up for him.

"You'll need to get on the radio and call in a preliminary description of the shooter," I said. "Mexican-American male, approximately 25-35, wearing a black baseball cap and a white or pale blue shirt. He screeched away from here in a Yellow, number one, zero, four, one, hit at least one car out on Thirty-eighth Street and headed west."

The young patrolman was thin and wore a handlebar moustache and a puzzled expression. He stared at my ID badge and then at me, but didn't say anything. He made no attempt to move either.

"Young man," I said. "You want to end your career, right here, right now?" I committed his name and badge number to memory. "The longer you delay, the colder that trail gets."

"No, sir. Yes, sir. Uhmm, ma'am."

He sprinted to his unit and grabbed his microphone.

Lord save us from rookies, I thought.

More cops arrived and the crime scene was blocked off with sawhorses and yellow tape.

After a quick briefing when she arrived, I told the investigating supervisor I'd help question the witnesses but she made it quite clear she didn't need my help. She was younger than me, and although I'd seen her around I'd never worked with her before. I'd heard she was a bit of a hard-ass and she didn't do anything that would dispel that rumor with me. Some women officers get carried away with their *watch me—I can do anything attitude.*

Since I had to work extra hard to get ahead myself, I understood where she was coming from, but I didn't think her way would ever win friends or earn promotions. No skin off my nose, I thought and told her I'd be inside if she needed me.

I found a pay phone, called Lieutenant Hamilton. Harry Albright had just walked in he said and turned on his speakerphone. I gave them the brief story but included Avery's admission of his romp with Tami Louise the night she died.

"Will Peppard survive?" asked Hamilton.

"I'm not sure. The bullet caught him in the upper chest and he's lost a lot of blood," I said. "If he lives, it will be only because the doctors got right to him. Lucky, he was at the hospital's front door."

"If you want to call that luck," Harry said. "Do *you* think Peppard killed Tami Louise?"

"His story had a ring of truth, Harry. I planned for you to talk to him. I wanted your opinion before making a final judgement. I didn't want to say—"

Hamilton interrupted, "Just a sec. I'm monitoring dispatch." I could hear a tinny voice in the background.

Hamilton said, "They found that cab, number 1041, abandoned at a supermarket parking lot just west of Seton. The driver was locked in the trunk. He's incoherent, but maybe we'll get a useful description when he calms down. Might even get some prints, but I doubt it."

"I'm coming over there, Zoe." Harry cleared his throat. "Maybe I can talk to Peppard when he gets out of surgery."

Hamilton said, "This town's just getting crazier."

"Reminds me of the good old days," said Harry.

I started to say something but Harry said, "You should have waited, Zoe, instead of going off half-cocked by yourself. You could have been hurt."

"Right, Harry. I'm sorry as hell you weren't here to protect me."

I heard Lieutenant Hamilton chortle in the background.

"Aw, you know what I mean," he said. "If my partner gets shot, I'd have to spend a half-day on the paperwork."

"Life's a bitch, Harry." I replaced the receiver and turned. Jason Foxx was right in my face. "What are you doing here?"

"Funny," he said, "that was my question."

"You first."

"My man on Peppard lost him this morning. I'd worked the six p.m. to six a.m. stakeout. He called and woke me up about thirty minutes ago when he'd done all he knew to find him." His eyes were bloodshot, and his curly red hair looked like someone had taken an eggbeater to it.

"I cruised around and listened to APD dispatch on my scanner," he continued. "A few minutes ago they gave a report of a shooting at Seton and your name came up. Don't know why I suspected—call it a hunch. Is it . . . ?"

"It's Peppard," I said. "Things look grim. I'm on my way to surgery now to check on his status."

"Are you going to tell me why you and Peppard were here at Seton Medical Center?"

"No can do," I said, speaking more harshly than I intended but added in a softer, firmer tone. "Officially I can't tell you squat. And right now, I'd like to know whether Peppard is dead or alive."

"Zoe?" Foxx caught my arm as I turned. "Don't forget, I'm on the same side as you." His voice was gentle.

"Of course you are." I moved forward. When his hand pulled away it left a warm tingle.

I ignored the warmth and walked to the central corridor, turned left and headed down the hall to the surgical suite. Foxx followed, hurrying to walk beside me and I felt guilty. "I didn't mean to be rude," I said. "It's just that things have escalated."

"I understand. Sorry I pressed," he said, sounding like he meant it. "I know how it is. Do you mind if I tag along? Peppard *is* still my client."

"Only to the waiting room up here. I'm going back into surgery."

When I reached the double swinging doors that have red signs with white letters stating NO ADMITTANCE Surgical Dept. I pushed the flat hand button that opens the doors and walked down the corridor.

A nurse stopped me before I'd gone too far and after flashing my badge and waiting, I managed to find out

Peppard was doing fine in surgery and that the doctor would talk to me when he sent his patient to recovery.

I'd just walked back to the waiting room and answered Foxx's quizzical look with a shrug when Kyle Raines showed up.

"You okay, Zoe?" Kyle asked. "The loot sent me. How's the vic?" He was into his TV cop show mode.

"A nurse told me Mr. Peppard is holding his own."

"Albright was on the radio when I came inside, said his ETA's two minutes," Kyle said. "He asked me to tell you to wait until he gets here before trying to talk to Peppard."

"I doubt we'll get to see him before tomorrow."

When Harry arrived I filled him in, and he said we'd been asked to go talk to Mrs. Peppard. "Oh?" I couldn't read his expression.

"She hasn't been told about the shooting yet. A patrol car went by the house to notify her but no one was at home. Supposedly they've called several times since then and only the answering machine picks up."

"Great," I said. "She doesn't know about her husband unless she knew the hit was supposed to go down today. And if she does know the guy who tried the hit, she's probably already left the country. That's what I'd do."

Without warning, my heart began racing and I could feel it pound against my chest wall. Moments later, my throat tightened and it felt like I couldn't breathe. I felt a sheen of perspiration coat my body and I'm sure I turned pale.

Harry noticed, although, I don't think the others did. He stepped closer and took my arm and whispered, "Let's get out of here. Over to the grieving widow."

"I planned to stay until he got out of surgery so I could talk to the doctor."

Kyle Raines said go ahead that he'd stay. Jason Foxx offered to wait with Kyle. I could tell from Kyle's face he wasn't too pleased about the P.I.'s company, but he didn't say anything.

My panic attack or whatever was nearly over when Harry and I got outside. "Wow. That's never happened before, I'm embarrassed to death."

"Don't be. It was a delayed adrenaline reaction to the trauma. Also it reminded you of when your husband was shot. I'd be worried about you if you didn't feel anything."

Probably right about the adrenaline, as far as the reminder of Byron's injury, I thought that idea ludicrous. "Ham loaned me his car," I said. "Why don't we take it to Peppard's?"

"You don't like my driving or what?"

"Let's just say I've had about all the excitement I can stand for one day."

We walked to the Thunderbird, got in and I started the engine. "You got an address?"

"Westlake Hills." Harry opened his notebook and read the street address aloud.

Twenty minutes later we were at Peppard's house. Harry rang the front doorbell, but no one responded. We went to the back where I knocked with the same result.

"A side door on the deck around here is cracked open," said Harry from the corner of the house. "Place kinda looks deserted."

I followed Harry around on the east side and we stood and peered through the quarter-inch crack of a patio glass door into what was obviously the master bedroom. Some clothing, one shoe, a purse and some papers were scattered around the floor and bed.

"Vandals maybe?" Harry asked.

"Or else she's a messy housekeeper," I said, spotting a pair of panty hose and a couple of bras dangling from a chair back.

"Maybe we should take a quick look around." Harry

pushed the door open approximately two inches, but not enough to enter.

"What grounds you going to use to justify going in?" I asked.

"We've got probable cause with Peppard just being shot." He slid the door a little more with his foot.

I was behind him and leaning around his shoulder to see.

Harry pointed to a doorway, presumably the bath, off to his left. "Hey, does that look like blood to you?"

I shielded my eyes from the outside glare and looked. On the white tile floor were some spatters and droplets of what actually did bear a remarkable resemblance to blood. "Maybe she cut herself shaving."

"Hey, Peppard just got shot. We came over to notify the missus. The patio door's cracked open and the place looks vandalized. She could be lying in there dead or something. I think I'd be remiss if I didn't go in for a better look."

"Do you want me to call for back-up?" I asked.

"Let's see what we have first. Might not be necessary." He walked the few feet to the bathroom and squatted for a closer look.

I pulled my gun out to cover him and stepped just inside the door's threshold. "Maybe she and the boyfriend got into a fight when the shooter missed."

Harry grunted.

"Although how would he know he hadn't killed Avery?" I said and thought some more. "Something made her leave in a hurry. Maybe he called to say he's shot Avery and they got into it or something."

Harry wasn't paying any attention to my speculations or else he hadn't heard me.

"No doubt in my mind," he said. "It's not much, but it's definitely blood."

On Oct. 14, 1930, a gravel runway alongside a one-room office was dedicated and named Robert Mueller Airport in honor of a former city councilman. The announced regular flight schedule? One northbound flight every morning and one southbound flight every afternoon—weather permitting. (Compiled from: the Austin History Center Records.)

Chapter 14

"Harry, that's not enough blood to worry about. Looks more like it was a nosebleed to me."

"I agree. Not enough blood for a search warrant."

"You want me to search the house?" I asked.

He stood and looked at me. "Who do you think you are with that gun? Annie Oakley?"

"It's called looking out for your partner's backside. Someone might still be in here."

"Believe me, this place is as empty as a Baptist church on Saturday night," he said.

"How do you know?" I put my gun back in its fanny pack holster.

"Stand still and listen. Breathe in the air. There." He exhaled. "Feel it."

"Whatever." Occupied houses holding felons were more my speed and that's where I usually looked for bad guys to arrest. Once inside an occupied house we wanted these bad guys quickly down on the floor, and in handcuffs so that no one was a threat. Things were different in homicide. I'd have to learn to think in a new way.

I did as he said, however, listening and breathing. In a moment or two, I sensed what Harry meant. This house *was* empty.

"Why don't you check this room, Zoe? Being a woman you should be able—"

"Aw cripes, Harry, don't turn sexist on me."

"All I was going to say," he had a sarcastic tone, "before you so rudely interrupted me, is that a woman can tell much easier what another woman has packed." He glanced at the mess. "Has she moved out? Or is this just a weekend trip?"

"Sorry. I'm never sure what's in your mind, old man."

Geez, I thought, now I'm being ageist. Okay, things like that can slip out; I didn't have to make an issue out of every little word the man uttered. "Uh, just watch out, okay?"

Harry grunted and headed down the hallway.

I opened my urban pack, which also holds my gun, took out and slipped on a pair of surgical gloves. The pack also holds handcuffs, evidence bag and my police ID and badge. White walls with black carpets and black furniture—a high-tech-looking decor that looked more like office than a bedroom to me. The high rectangular windows without drapes or blinds added to that illusion.

Avery's influence, I thought, since he's a software maven. Two huge his-n-hers closets took up one wall.

I peeked in hers. Chock full of designer clothes and shoes but one shoe rack had two empty spots. The lady definitely packed light for someone with such abundance. A random thought occurred—maybe she'd just walked out and left everything.

That could make sense if she anticipated a couple of million in insurance money. She well might have great shopping plans. But would she leave all her old stuff?

I wouldn't. And I'd almost bet Mrs. Peppard would take her favorite Versace and Donna Karan.

I checked the bathroom and found enough make-up, perfume and cosmetics to make me feel she probably hadn't moved out. "Where have you gone, Mary Margaret?" I wondered aloud.

Back in the bedroom I pawed through the trash on the floor: wadded-up facial tissues, a drugstore receipt for two pairs of L'Egg's Sheer Energy panty hose, a small box that one pair of hose came in, the paper insert from inside the package, and two envelopes. Both envelopes were empty—one was from Franklin Savings Bank and the other from a travel agency.

Harry walked in. "Empty house. Just like I said. Find anything?"

I gathered up the trash, placing it on the bed and the significance of the travel agency envelope registered. "Looks like she's flown the coop, but we might find out something from these people." I handed Harry the envelope, and threw the rest in a wastebasket.

"I saw a phone book in the kitchen," he said. "I'll give them a call. Then we'd better leave; we are trespassing you know."

I knew he'd spoken, but I didn't hear him, because I'd just found what we needed wadded up in a tiny ball inside the trash basket. It was that funny onionskin-like paper favored by many travel agencies that caught my eye. I unrolled it. Sure enough, an itinerary for Mrs. Peppard and a Mr. Joe Arnold. The flight was with ConWorld Air, leaving at eight for Mexico City with an open return. No doubt Arnold was her lover. And the best part was—the flight was scheduled for tonight, which meant they hadn't left yet. Which meant we could stop them.

"Hey, Harry. Hold up! I got it right here."

Harry met me in the hallway.

"Maybe we don't know where Mary Margaret Peppard is right now, but we sure as hell know where she'll be at eight o'clock tonight."

Harry gave me a high five.

I made a final circuit through the house trying to get a feel for Mrs. Peppard. The living room furniture of brass and chrome and glass gave it a high-tech office look also. The wooden trim on the tables was light colored so as not to detract from the metallic stuff, I supposed. The room's only color came from several abstract paintings and a few bright pillows on an off-white sofa.

The family room walls were paneled in light oak except for one wall wholly devoted to shelves of all different lengths and sizes. A fifty-inch TV screen was in the exact center of the shelving, its dark face looking like a black window to nowhere.

One short shelf held photographs, but only one was of Avery and a woman I assumed was Mrs. Peppard. A studio-made bust shot probably taken about the time they were married, I thought, and tried to remember if he said they'd been married one or two years.

Mary Margaret looked like a college girl—maybe only a few years older—more like Avery's daughter than his wife.

She was lovely, although her thick blonde hair seemed to weigh down her small head. I looked at the face of the woman who seemed to want to commit murder to get out of a bad marriage.

She didn't look like a murderer, but does anyone?

I slipped the photo out of the frame in case we needed to make copies.

When we returned to homicide, Harry filled in the Lieutenant on what we'd discovered while I got on the telephone to verify the reservations with ConWorld and to double check the flight times.

Then I borrowed Harry's computer to run Mary Margaret's name. The only pertinent information to pop out was the fact her maiden name was Arnold. Running an inquiry on Joe Arnold turned up nothing. Most likely it was a phony maiden name.

I wondered if the trip had been scheduled to give her an

alibi? Surely she could figure out if her husband was murdered, she'd be a suspect. The spouse is almost always looked at first. If so, why had the hit gone down before the plane left?

Harry came back to his desk and said his boss would get an arrest warrant for Mrs. Peppard.

"For what? She didn't shoot him."

"Conspiracy works for me. But if not, we can pick her up for questioning."

"I called the hospital, they've upgraded Avery to good," I said. "We can probably talk to him later tonight unless we get tied up with the missus."

"He'll keep. He probably saw less than you did." Harry looked uncomfortable. I was sitting in his chair, which most likely was molded to his bottom. So I got up and sat opposite him.

The arrest warrants arrived a little after four and Harry and I stopped off at Wendy's for hamburgers and fries since we'd missed lunch and had a couple of hours to kill.

"This case gets weirder the more you think about it." I stuffed some potatoes into my mouth.

"How so?" Harry asked. He was scarfing food at about the same rate I was. Neither of us knew when we'd have time to eat again.

"If I had hired a hit man to kill my spouse, I'd get my carcass out of town prior to the shooting so I could have an alibi. It doesn't make any sense otherwise."

"That's what you or I would do, because we're smart enough to figure it out. No one has ever said bad guys are playing with a full deck. And I agree something else seems out of whack."

"Okay, if you were a hitter—why would you take someone out in such a public place? Especially a target who's easy to find. There's too many places without witnesses around."

"Avery was jumpy. Maybe he made the hitter jumpy, too."

"Jason Foxx was supposed to be tailing Avery. Maybe the hitter spotted Foxx and got nervous. So when the opportunity presented itself—it was too good a chance to pass up."

"Nope. Something made them jump the gun, I just don't know what," said Harry. "Homicide always makes sense to a killer, but it never makes sense to me."

"Foxx told me he was asleep and his man lost Peppard this morning. Could *he* have been trying for an alibi?"

"Good question for which I have no answer." Harry looked at his watch. "We need to be on our way if we want to set things up with the airport police."

As we pulled out of Wendy's, he said, "Maybe we'll get some answers when we pick up Mrs. Peppard and this Joe Arnold."

"Yeah, whoever that is."

Harry turned into the road leading to the main gate. "You been out here often?"

"Only three or four times. I haven't had many opportunities since Byron was hurt."

Robert Mueller Airport served Austin many years but Austin's growing population demanded expansion. Since Mueller was too close to downtown there was no room to grow. Plans for a new airport continued until finally a decision was made.

The new Austin-Bergstrom International airport is unique by any standard. Its crescent shape offers room for expansion and is expected to meet Austin's needs well into the new century. Bergstrom had a fifty-two year history as a military airbase beginning in 1941. "Eight days before Pearl Harbor," Harry said, "the U.S. Army talked city officials into agreeing to build this base. A land site didn't get chosen for nine months, however."

"Do you know who it was named for?" I asked. Harry shook his head. "Captain John Bergstrom, the first Austinite killed in the war. He went down at Clark Field in the Phillippines."

"How do you know that?"

"History was a passion of my dad. That's one of those trivia facts I remember."

Bergstrom's past included being both a strategic and a tactical command base, participating in the Berlin air lifts after WWII and continued by sending jet sorties in the Gulf War and during Desert Storm. Its fate as a military base ended with the military downsizing acts and the Stars and Stripes were struck for the last time in 1993.

Austin is proud to be a live music capital and ABI boasts a music stage in the center of the terminal where a variety of soul, rock, jazz, country, blues, classical, folk and pop may be heard.

The food places featuring Austin specialties are Salt Lick or Harlon's Barbeque, Matt's Famous El Rancho, Armadillo Café and Amy's Ice Cream. All restaurants are strung along the crescent-shape so that almost every gate has food nearby.

The airport police department is not part of the Austin City police but they work closely with APD when necessary. They're also city employees. Harry and I met a Sergeant Hazel Richards, the ranking officer on duty in the chief's office where we identified ourselves and explained the situation. An older woman about my size with gray hair swept back into a chignon, she had a faint line of dark hair above her lip and a nose that hooked slightly on the end. She was rather plain and reminded me of my second-grade teacher, Mrs. Kingsley. She called together her crew and briefed them in a no-nonsense tone. We made copies of the photo I had of Mrs. Peppard and gave them to each officer including the checkpoint folks who work for another entity—a private security firm.

Flight 86 originated in Arizona, made stops in Austin and Houston before going on to Mexico City. The ConWorld personnel were happy to cooperate but for now, all they could say was that our quarry had not canceled their flight.

By seven p.m. Harry and I were in position at ConWorld's Gate 7, posing as gate crew personnel. The eight o'clock flight was scheduled to leave from Gate 5. The waiting area started to fill with departing folks and included a small group waiting to meet the incoming flight from Arizona.

I watched as three stair-step-sized children, ages three to six, laughingly chased each other around a support column near a check-in counter. They were having a good time and not bothering anyone, but their mother kept saying "Settle down, now. Settle down." The children, of course, ignored her.

An old man, using a walker, arrived with two women. The older one tried not to look as if she was hurrying him along and the younger one looked as if she'd rather be anywhere else.

Nervous anticipation made me jittery. I had no idea why, but I felt something would go terribly wrong and I couldn't shake the feeling. Maybe the roomful of innocent people worried me.

I searched women's faces hoping to spot someone who looked like Mrs. Peppard. Finally, Harry took me by the arm and led me across the waiting area over near a bank of pay telephones. We stood about twenty feet from the restroom entryways for each sex, next door to each other.

"You're acting like a rookie on her first stake-out, Zoe. You're going to give it all away unless you get under control."

"I know . . . uh, I can't explain it." I pulled the photo of

Mary Margaret up partway out of my purse and looked at it again.

"Look, she's just a rich lady who may have plotted to kill her husband," he said. "Neither she nor Arnold will be armed because they have to go through Charlie before coming up here."

"I know, and we're just picking her up for questioning, right? But why does the hair on the back of my neck keep squirming?"

"Feelings like that should be acknowledged," he said. "Why don't we go get our Kevlar vests? Might make you feel better." He started down the corridor.

"Okay." I thought about it a moment. "But let's just—"

A tinny-sounding voice came over the walkie-talkie Harry had been given by the airport police. "Post three, report immediately to Gate 6." That code signified the suspect had arrived.

I'd kept half an eye on people as we talked and I'd seen no one who fit Mrs. Peppard's description in the vicinity.

A young African-American male, with a moon-shaped face and jug ears leaned on the counter at Gate 6. He wore a spotless airport police uniform and all five-feet-six inches of him looked competent, his wiry arms and muscular shoulders added to the picture. He introduced himself as Jordan Reed. "You see that young Hispanic woman over there by the window?" he asked.

"The one in the black leather skirt and the red boots?" I asked. A red long-sleeved blouse with a paisley vest completed her ensemble. Her black hair was loose, one side hanging behind her shoulder and the other side forward. She was pretty with delicate features and if she were old enough to vote I'd be surprised.

Reed nodded. "She just tried to check in as Mary

Margaret Peppard, but she didn't have a photo ID in that name."

"You've got to be kidding," said Harry.

"Doesn't look a bit like her picture," I said. "Wonder who she is? Any word on Joe Arnold?"

"Don't look now, Ms. Barrow," Reed said. "He's the guy walking toward the men's room."

Harry faced in that direction, but if I'd turned I'd have been too obvious. "Mexican-American," Harry said. "Around thirty, dressed in gray brushed jeans and a black turtle-necked sweater. 'Bout the size of Reed here, but taller. If he's a Joe Arnold, I'm Clint Eastwood."

"That's the name on the ticket he's using, but his Louisiana driver's license says Antonio Arno," said Reed. "Now you can turn around, Ms. Barrow, he's gone inside. When he comes back out you can see him."

"Zoe, why don't you go introduce yourself to the phony Ms. Peppard over there? I think Officer Reed and I might have a chat with Joe what's his face over in the men's room."

I grinned at them. "You sure y'all don't want my help?"

"Naw, we can handle it—" Harry realized I was teasing. "I ought to make you go in there by yourself," he said. "Except you'd probably get hurt and then I'd have to do all the paperwork."

"Right." I strolled over to the young woman. "Ms. Peppard?" She looked up and her face got a funny look when she realized I was speaking to her. "Ms. Peppard? I'm with airport security, I'd like to see some identification, please."

Her wide startled eyes darted to the men's room then back to me. "I, uh, I doan unnerstand. Why you want me?"

She peered at the bathroom door again, then out the window, down to the floor, and everywhere except at me.

"Just routine, Mrs. Peppard," I said.

"I'm, uh, I . . ." Her face suddenly crumpled and big tears overflowed the dark eyes and down her face. "You, uh . . . can't search me without a warrant, can you?"

"Ma'am, I don't want to search you, I'd just like to see something with your name on it—driver's license, credit card—anything that proves you're Mary Margaret Peppard."

I heard a commotion behind me and turned. A man ran out of the men's room. Splotched patches of pink were stark on his pale face. He hurried to a woman who leaned over the water fountain and gestured and looked back towards the bathroom.

As I moved in that direction, a Mexican-American male, fitting the description Reed had given us earlier, came through the door. His size and looks were similar to the man I'd seen drive away from Seton hospital. Aw hell, that's got to be the man who shot Avery, I thought.

He saw me. And in that one frozen instant, I'd swear I saw recognition in his face. But then he turned and started towards the front of the airport walking at a fast clip.

I moved quickly after him and pulled out my walkie-talkie. "Harry? Harry? Are you okay?"

No answer.

The phony Mrs. Peppard began to scream. "Tony? Where you goin'?"

This end of the hallway stretches towards the building's central entrance and edged all along the way are airline gates, newsstands, gift shops, restaurants and bars. The guy half-walked-half-jogged as he dodged people.

How did this guy get away from Harry? I spoke into the walkie-talkie again. "Harry? Answer me please."

Nothing but dead air. What the heck? Surely Harry was okay and following the man was foremost. I pushed the all channel button and heard a garbled voice in the static.

"You're break . . . (squawk) . . . Whatcha got?"

"I'm in pursuit of a suspect and need back-up." I gave a quick description of the suspect and that he was heading to the main entrance. "Officers may be down and need help in men's room at Gate 6." I pulled out my badge, holding it above my head as I switched from a jog to a run.

"Police officer," I said. "Move out of the way, please."

Some people complained and one man even cussed me out. I'll remember you, I thought. "Police officer coming through. Excuse me." My quarry neared the security point and I lost him for a minute behind a group of people streaming out from one of the gates.

A big man running towards the departing gates creamed me and sent the walkie-talkie flying.

"Sorry, lady," the man said. "I'm late."

"Next time start earlier," I said but by then he was out of earshot.

I wasted no time looking for the walkie-talkie. A dimestore variety and worthless. A huge crowd surrounded the music stage as a group performed a smooth-jazz number.

I wondered why the guards at Checkpoint Charlie hadn't intercepted my suspect, but when I asked two of them to come with me, we spotted the suspect running down the up escalator. The escalator led to the lower floor and baggage claim turnstiles. I hopped on the down escalator and the guards followed.

One guard gave me his walkie-talkie and that's when I discovered the checkpoint security guards were on an entirely different channel. No wonder they hadn't heard my earlier call.

As I got off the escalator a sharp muscle spasm knifed into my side and bent me double. One of those things you called a "stitch" when you were a kid. I slowed for a moment—scanning the crowd but couldn't spot the suspect. I tried to walk but the pain was excruciating. I had to stop.

Suddenly I saw a guy in a security uniform run out a door marked "EMPLOYEES ONLY" and an alarm was ringing. The suspect must have bolted and set off the alarm.

Then an excited voice came from the radio. "We got him, we got him. He ran right into our arms." And then a moment later, "We're taking him into the chief's office." I couldn't see them anywhere, but had to take their word for it.

I straightened and tried to breathe. As soon as I could talk again, I called Harry on the correct radio channel, and this time he answered back.

"Zoe? I'm okay. Can you hear me? I just got my breath knocked out. I'm not sure about Reed, yet. Where's the little s.o.b.?"

"They caught him." I needed to get back up to ConWorld's gate to check on my partner and Reed, but I was really tired. I spotted and quickly commandeered one of the golf carts and drivers who are available to transport physically challenged people to the gates.

The phony Mrs. Peppard had followed the chase partway down. She was slumped against the wall, crying and when I told her to join me on the cart she asked if I knew why Tony had left.

"I have no idea," I told her as we reached the gate areas. The driver stopped next to the men's room.

"You sit right there." I slipped my handcuffs on her and hooked her to the cart. I walked inside the men's room, hoping Harry and Reed could explain themselves.

"You have the right to remain silent," the words begin. The Supreme Court mandated the Miranda warnings on June 13, 1966, by ruling in Miranda v Arizona that the defendant was not adequately informed of his rights before interrogation. (Compiled from: Austin History Center Records: *Austin American Statesman Monthly Almanac.*)

Chapter 15

A disheveled Harry struggled with Officer Reed at the lavatory basin. Blood ran from Reed's nose, splotching his crisp blue uniform shirt.

"You okay, Harry?" I asked.

"Yeah. Got the wind knocked out, that's all." He got Reed situated and turned on the water. "Guy kicked Reed in the face—probably broke his nose. I know he passed out briefly."

Reed bent over and splashed his face but he muttered curses with every other breath.

Harry patted Reed on the back. "You okay, boss?"

"Hell, yes," said Reed. "Ain't the first time this old honker's been broke. Probably won't be the last. How're you doing, Harry?"

"I'm fine." Harry rubbed his diaphragm. "Guy came out of the stall when I was looking into the next one. He punched Reed and when I jumped him, he got me right in the solar plexus."

He made Reed let him look at the nose. "It's jammed over to one side, a doctor needs to fix it."

Reed leaned over the lavatory again as the blood flow began anew.

Harry's voice was gruff. "And just where were you while all this was going on? Did you even catch the slime bag?"

That ornery so and so. How dare he! "What do you think I was doing? Out taking a stroll?"

"I thought maybe you stopped off to get your nails done or your hair fluffed. I know how some women are—always worried about their appearance."

"Yeah, right. And I got my toenails painted while the airport cops caught him. Sergeant Richards will detain him until we get there and transport him downtown."

"Good. I'd like to have a few words with him. Alone."

"Did you bring your rubber hose along?" I asked, but he and Reed were too busy laughing and telling each other what they'd like to do to the guy. None of it was pleasant.

He could be infuriating, but there was one piece of information I wanted him to know. "Harry," I said, "I'm pretty sure this is the guy who shot Avery Peppard."

"But you can't make a positive ID, can you?" Harry pulled a comb from his back pocket and ran it through his hair.

"I'd be willing to say so in court, but we need hard evidence."

"I'll get it. Don't you even worry about that."

"If Reed here's doing okay, we should go and—"

Reed assured us he'd be fine. "Go ahead," he said. "I'll be along in a couple more minutes."

Harry patted me on the back. "I was only teasing you about goofing around. I'm sure you did your part to catch lover-boy."

"It's okay, Harry. But if you hadn't let him best you to begin with. I know how older guys hate to admit they're slowing down. But don't worry. I'll keep your little secret."

Reed laughed and Harry looked ready to throttle me for a moment, then smiled. "Okay," he said, "Mark one up for the female."

Before I could say anything, two men came hurrying inside—one right behind the other, both with a hand on a zipper. I turned and they each did a double take, whirled around and walked out. I'd forgotten that I stood in the men's room. "Guess they're the shy types," I said over my shoulder as I walked out the door.

I unhooked the female suspect from the cart. "We need to have a little talk downtown."

"I no know nothin'," she whined. "Tony just called today and ask me to go on this trip."

"Then you have nothing to hide and can tell me all about it and what you know about Tony."

When we arrived at her office, Sergeant Hazel Richards was all smiles. "Reed just radioed that he's stopped bleeding and thinks he's going to live."

"You guys do good work," I said and meant it. "Where's our suspect?"

"In my office with two men watching him."

We had the young woman sit in the reception area with an officer. We didn't want her and the guy together. Too easy to cook up some story if they had time alone.

A short time later, two squad cars arrived to take our detainees downtown. When Harry and a patrol officer brought her boyfriend out from the inner office, the young woman suspect began screaming at him in Spanish. He screamed back—also in Spanish.

It's hard to live in Texas without picking up a little Tex-Mex, but he spoke so rapidly and my knowledge was so limited, I didn't know what he was saying.

Sergeant Richards, who could speak and understand the lingo, said "Tony" was telling the girl she'd better keep her fat mouth shut else he'd shut it for her. The remainder of his tirade, as they led him outside, was curses and disparaging remarks about everyone's ancestry. That part I understood.

Richards patted down the young woman and then the patrol officer took off my handcuffs. She was cursing and crying as she left.

Officer Reed showed up and despite his protests was soon convinced to go to a nearby emergency clinic. We thanked Richards and her staff and headed downtown.

Our invited guests were placed in separate interrogation rooms awaiting our arrival. Harry introduced me to his boss, Lieutenant Hector Olivera, who looked amazingly like that Hispanic hunk actor Jimmy Smits, except shorter, and we gave him a quick version of what had happened.

Olivera explained that "Tony," as the girl called him, had a Texas driver's license with the name of Anthony Garcia. Since that name is about as common as John Smith in the Anglo community, Olivera said he was running a computer check to see if Tony was legal.

Harry got coffee for both of us while Olivera conferred with an officer who had done preliminary questioning of the young woman.

"Tony claims he found the airline tickets," said Olivera. "We've identified the woman as Connie Mendoza. She swears she knows nothing—that Tony had only asked her along for the ride."

Then Olivera smiled a sweet-briar-eating, satisfied jackass sort of smile. "Sergeant Richards out at the airport pulled their luggage and guess what she found?"

"Something to tie him into the hit on Peppard, I hope," said Harry.

"A three-fifty-seven Magnum and all's we're waiting on now is a ballistics report," Olivera said. "The bullet dug out of Peppard is already at the lab, so it shouldn't take long."

"If it's a match, is that enough to charge him?" I asked.

"You bet your sweet ass," said Harry.

"Now your questions will have some teeth," said Olivera. "Be sure to Mirandize him again, Harry. I don't want any reverse rulings."

"You want to do it, Hec?" Harry asked. "My Spanish's a bit rusty."

"What about his lawyer?" I asked.

Olivera looked at me. "Oh, he's already asking for his phone call. He's not going to say anything until then, but we've got him by the short hairs."

Olivera, Harry and I walked into the room where Tony Garcia sat waiting. He turned pale for a moment when he saw us, then began looking down and around as if searching for a trap door.

Harry read him his rights in English and Olivera recited it in Spanish. "Do you understand these rights?"

Garcia nodded and mocked Harry using the same tone. "Yeah, I understand."

"Well, just so's there won't be problems later," said Harry and Olivera read the Miranda again.

Garcia grinned the whole time and answered. "Si, mon capitan." And then he asked for a lawyer. Olivera left the room.

"Do you have a lawyer?" Harry asked.

Garcia said he did and a telephone was brought in, plugged in and Garcia dialed a number.

Garcia's lawyer said he would be over in about thirty minutes. Harry and I went out to his desk to wait.

"Did you see him blanch when you and I walked in?" I asked.

"Yeah. Wonder why?"

"Maybe he was afraid you were going to pay him back for what he did to you at the airport."

"Wonder if I could make his nose match Reed's if I used a rubber hose?"

"Harry, you're so baaaad. And I'm beginning to think you have a one-track mind. You and that rubber hose."

"You're the one who keeps bringing it up."

Olivera walked out of the room where the girl was waiting and asked if we wanted to talk to her while we waited for Garcia's lawyer to arrive. "She hasn't been arrested and says she'll cooperate. I think she's just a kid who got caught in something she doesn't know or understand."

Olivera said she didn't have a rap sheet.

"I doubt she knows anything," said Harry.

"She could know something significant and not even know it," I said. "Let's talk to her anyway."

Harry grumbled, but followed along.

In less than five minutes we were sure Connie Mendoza knew only what Tony had told her. "I want to clear this up," she said. "Tony said his boss gave him the airline tickets and told him to take along a lady friend."

"Which doesn't jibe with the lost and found tale," I said in a quiet tone to Harry.

Connie claimed she didn't know who Tony's boss was and she'd never heard of Mary Margaret Peppard or Joe Arnold. She'd known Tony about a week and had only agreed to go along because Tony had promised her a great weekend. "Some weekend, huh?" she said.

"Maybe next time you'll be more choosy about who you travel with Connie," I said.

She continued to answer our questions fully and without hesitation.

After a few more minutes we agreed she had probably done nothing wrong, and Harry said he'd tell Olivera we recommend sending Connie home.

Someone stood in Olivera's office with a batch of papers talking animatedly. We headed for the break room for coffee. Five minutes later, Olivera walked up and said he wanted to talk to me in his office.

I raised an eyebrow at Harry, but kept my mouth shut. And so did Harry.

Olivera handed Harry a file and said, "When you've read this, come join us."

I followed Olivera down to his office. He waited until I was inside, then closed the door. He motioned me to a chair and sat down behind his desk. He leaned back in his chair, folded both arms across his chest and looked at me. During all this time not a word was spoken.

I had no earthly idea what was going on and I knew from Harry's expression when I left him, he was in the dark, too. If Olivera was going to fill me in, why was he taking so long to get started? Maybe he just didn't know how, I thought, and as if reading my thoughts, he began.

"Zoe," said Olivera. "I'm not exactly sure how it all connects but I just found out some interesting news about Anthony Garcia. He was released from Huntsville four weeks ago. I gave Harry Garcia's record to read."

"What was he in for?"

"This time for aggravated assault. He beat a hooker severely last year and served thirteen months of a ten-year sentence."

"He got paroled?"

"Yes. Model prisoner, time off for good behavior—the whole nine yards."

"But now we have attempted murder and this is his third felony. This time he's looking at twenty-five to life."

Olivera grimaced. I could tell he was disturbed, but I didn't know him well enough to read beyond that. "Something else's bothering you," I said, making it a statement rather than a question.

"Yes, but let's wait until Harry comes in to discuss it."

"Fine." I didn't know what else to say. I was totally baffled.

Harry walked in sixty seconds later and now he was the one who had the disturbed look in his eyes.

Harry looked at me, then blurted, "Goddamit, Zoe, you were the target all along—not Peppard."

"What do you mean, I was the target?" I stared at Harry, watched him shrug, then looked at Olivera and back at Harry once again. "I was there. His first bullet went wild. The second hit Avery Peppard right smack in the chest. The guy sure wasn't shooting straight if I was his target. But why would he want to shoot me? I never saw the guy before in my life."

"He's related to the man you shot to death. He's Jesse Garcia's uncle, Zoe," said Harry. "Tony was out to avenge Jesse."

Recent noteworthy happenings from an 1887 newspaper: all trains were on time yesterday and all reached Austin without being robbed. However a young man was charged with malicious mischief and fined $10. His crime? He killed a cow and had to pay for his fun. (Compiled from: *The Austin American Statesman Monthly Almanac.*)

Chapter 16

Usually I spent time with Byron at the nursing home after work and tonight was no different. Before going to his room, however, I stopped for a moment and talked to the registered nurse who worked the evening shift. Tommie Lou Herring was pushing sixty and she had one of those sweet faces that reminded you of your favorite grandmother. You could tell she was a caring nurse just by looking at her.

I asked about Byron's appetite, which was fair, and about his weight, which was unchanged. Tommie said Byron was grinding his teeth and she gave me the name of a dentist who made house visits at the nursing home. Tommie's telephone rang, I waved and walked on down the hall.

I settled myself in a chair next to the bed, and holding my husband's good hand, told him about Avery and Mary Margaret. He opened and closed his eyes, made a couple of weird grimaces with his face, but gave no sign that he recognized or heard me.

The nurse's aide on night duty, Lucy Lynn Johnstone, walked in and said hi. She's a short, but large-boned woman with a rose tattooed on her left arm. Her dark African-American hair was braided in cornrows. She looked formidable but her warm smile and heart of gold captured me in our early days of being here.

"Mr. Byron really complained at his bath tonight," Lucy said with a smile. "You should have heard him fussing at me."

"Really? What did he say?" I asked.

"Well, I couldn't understand the word, but the tone sounded like complaints to me."

"Then he probably was," I said. "He always was good at letting you know what he thought."

We chatted for a few moments and she left. I stayed for a time holding Byron's hand and when I went out into the empty night for home I felt like a gerbil going round and round in a wire treadmill. My life only went in circles and I couldn't seem to get off and go in another direction.

Melody and Lyric gave me an ecstatic welcome home and after we'd all had dinner and a bath—mine in the shower and theirs by their little pink tongues—we watched the David Letterman Show together and went to bed, also together. They like to curl up at my feet.

The next day Harry's boss told him the Peppard investigation was at a standstill and to let up on the Tami Louise Smuts case, too. Harry protested, but there were other more important and more recent murders to solve. Tami Louise was just another dead hooker and the thinking was that she'd been killed during some drug deal gone bust. Her killer would turn up sooner or later, plea-bargaining the information to get a reduced sentence on his current charges. Some days police work consists of nothing much, unfortunately those days are few and far between nowadays.

I was to report immediately back to my department. My team was working a case on a newly discovered speed lab and I was needed.

Harry Albright and I met for lunch. "Harry, I enjoyed working with you."

"Stick around, kid, we might do it again some time. Just so you know, I plan to keep working on Miss Smutt's case on my own time."

I raised an eyebrow at him.

"I told you I don't like killers in my town and I don't ever give up."

"Thanks, Harry. I'm glad there's guys like you around." Several cold cases had been solved recently by officers who continued to rework leads. "Harry? Can you use my help in any way?"

"Sure. I'll call you tonight and we can discuss a plan I have." He smiled and as I paid for our lunch, his smile grew bigger.

Anthony Garcia was arraigned and a high bail had been set. Mary Margaret Peppard had not yet been found. Neither had her mysterious lover.

Harry and I had discussed the implications of Anthony Garcia's attempt on Avery Peppard—whether I had really been the target, not Avery, or whether Garcia had been paid to kill Avery. If so, who? It was one complicated puzzle to me. Garcia hadn't talked and I felt he never would unless somehow we found a crack in his satisfied life to shake him.

Garcia's whole attitude gave a fresh meaning to some quirky throwback gene from Old Testament dogma, "An Eye for an Eye," seeking an imagined family honor or some such. But how and where did the Peppards fit in, if they did? And they had to fit somewhere. Otherwise Garcia wouldn't have had Mrs. Peppard's airline tickets.

Neither Harry nor I reached any conclusions and we knew it would take a deeper investigation to find out what was really at the bottom of this whole thing. Without viable leads we were stymied. Harry's boss wanted him to work on more current cases.

That evening I stopped by Seton Hospital and checked on Peppard. He was much improved and would be released the next morning. His room was full of visitors so I didn't stop in to talk although I recognized Jean Barrow, my mother-in-law, along with her sister, Susan, who was Avery's ex-wife. Forgive and forget? I wondered.

A quick stop over Lianne's house found her feeling great and holding court with a group of fellow officers including Kyle Raines. She and Kyle gave each other long glances and when they touched accidentally their bodies seemed electrified. I could tell they were escalating straight into a relationship and the idea worried me. I didn't judge them, but after about ten minutes of watching, I pleaded fatigue and left.

Was I jealous? I didn't think so. Lianne *is* my friend and I worried about her. She and I have been together for some of the best and worst times of our lives. We've fought the wars against the prejudice of women in APD. Not only was public perception a problem, some male officers thought we were only useful to play decoy hookers or helped smoke out rapists.

Anything else—homicide, special missions, narcotics, even riding patrol alone—was thought to be too dangerous for women. She and I, along with a few others worked diligently to change that perception. One big advantage we had through it all was the fact that the city of Austin has historically been a progressive city. The citizens are academics, political and high-tech people, all mixed in with the farmers, cowboys, and oilmen and thrown together with the creative artists, musicians and literary types. Folks move here from everywhere and it makes for a wonderful global diversity. That attitude had opened many doors for women, including our own governor's office—we certainly made Ann Richards a household name.

Lianne's always been there for me and when I realized Byron would never get well, I'd leaned heavily on that friendship. I wouldn't desert her, but her proclivity for bad relationships are legendary. And if Kyle's wife ever found out, I'd do my part to keep my friend on an even keel. Meanwhile, I worried and vowed to keep my mouth shut.

When I got home, Harry called. "Garcia is out."

"No way."

"He escaped when they transferred him to County. I want you to be extra careful, Zoe."

"I'll bet you money he's already half way to Mexico."

"Probably. Do you want me to come over?"

I assured him I could manage. "He doesn't know where I live, Harry. I'm okay here." He grunted and disconnected abruptly.

I took a huge plate of macaroni salad out on the deck and ate while watching Melody and Lyric play a game of tag. Fretting about Lianne added to the week's events: Avery getting shot, the stake-out at the airport for Mary Margaret, chasing Tony Garcia and learning that I may have been his target. Now to hear he had escaped added up to a lot of stress for one tired policewoman. The nearby water of Town Lake and a cold beer after I'd put a little food inside my body was the perfect antidote for what ailed me.

The day metamorphosed into night, equally glorious in spring-like qualities. The sky was clear, and although the brightness of the midtown lights all but wiped out the night sky, there were two or three stars bright enough to be seen if you knew where to look, and if you turned out the porch light and the two security lights on this side of the building, which I did. After a little while my eyes adjusted to the semi-blackness and, sure enough, I noted a couple other stars. The moon wasn't up yet.

It was cool enough for a sweater and I had an afghan to put over my feet. The weather news I'd heard at ten p.m. told of another snowstorm blanketing the Midwestern part of the country and the 60-degree February evening in central Texas gave me only the smallest twinges of guilt.

Byron intruded on my thoughts as I pushed everything

else aside. Sometimes I felt so unconnected from him, entirely normal, I know, and when I was being totally honest with myself I knew it would never ever be any different. Jesse Garcia's bullet to my husband's head had changed everything. My life with Byron was over and the sooner I accepted that fact the better off I'd be. But it wasn't always easy to admit to that harsh reality.

"A nickel for your thoughts," a familiar male voice said, and I jumped about two feet into the air.

Jason Foxx's pale face beamed at me over the top rail of the deck. "Damn, Jason. You scared me out of a week's growth." I think I was a bit more worried about Garcia than I had admitted.

"Sorry." He laughed. "I knocked, but you didn't hear it. Your car was here and I kind of thought you'd be out on the deck. May I?" He put one foot and leg over the banister and paused.

"Come on," I said. He hopped over and pulled a lawn chair over next to my chaise. "You're willing to pay a whole nickel?" I asked.

"Inflation, you know. I thought it was a fair price for thoughts." When I didn't say anything, he reached into his pocket and held out a nickel. "Well?"

"God, I don't even know what I was thinking. Mostly just trying to unwind from a shitty week." I drained the last of my Coors Light and asked if he'd like one.

"Do you have the high-octane ones?"

"A regular Coors coming up." I stood, walked to the kitchen and got the beer, one for him and another Light for me. On the way outside, I switched the security lights back on but left the deck light off. The security lights were located just under the eaves and shone almost straight down, yet offered enough light to see someone's face. I like seeing someone's face when I'm talking to them.

Foxx popped the top on his can and said, "I heard you have a suspect in custody on the Peppard hit."

"We did. He's already out."

"How? I thought his bail would be set too high."

"It was, but he escaped during transfer from City Jail out to County. The parole board issued a blue warrant on him for parole violation. If they can find him and if he doesn't escape again, he won't be able to get out unless he's found not guilty when he's tried."

"Damn." Foxx cleared his throat. "I checked on Peppard tonight and he's much better."

"I know. He's going home tomorrow. Neither he nor anyone else has heard from Mary Margaret. He's filed a missing person on her." I stretched and yawned. "I feel sorry for him. He's a nice man and it's too bad he got caught up in a soap opera."

"And no one knows what's happened to his conniving wife?"

"She and her lover boy are obviously laying low. They'll show eventually, I guess."

"Did you get anything out of the shooter?"

"Are you getting nosy about my case?"

"Professional curiosity. Once a cop, always a cop."

"That's right. You were with Houston PD, weren't you?"

"Seventeen years."

"Why did you leave?" I'd wondered if he'd been fired or if he'd just suffered burnout. Harry had mentioned something to me about Foxx's background, but I'd forgotten the details.

"Too much politicking. I had to get out before I got suspended for mouthing off one time too many."

"I hear that, but you quit? Three years short of retirement?"

"Actually, it was medical. Shot in the line of duty."

I remembered then—Harry had said Foxx was injured in a gun battle with some crack dealer. The dealer didn't survive.

"How bad?" I asked. "I mean, you don't have any visible injuries." It dawned on me as I asked that his wound might not be in a location to discuss in mixed company and I blushed, grateful for the semi-darkness which I hoped hid my discomfort.

Jason Foxx laughed. "You want to see my scars?"

"God, no. Now I'm being the nosy one. Sorry."

"No problem." He slowly unbuttoned his shirt. When he had pulled it off, he stood, turning his back. "I lost my spleen."

I could see the jagged scars that ran halfway across his back and left side, from underneath his shoulder blade and even lower, going farther down and beneath the top of his Levi's. I also couldn't help noticing his broad shoulders and nice tight buns. The shadows playing across his skin made it looked tanned, even if it wasn't, and the darkness gave his red hair an auburn hue.

He looked sexy with his bared torso, a bit on the slender side yet muscular. I had always liked men with bared torsos, especially ones built like he was. But what scared the crud out of me was the butterflies churning in my stomach and tightness in my throat.

He turned slowly and tilted his head slightly, looking to see if it had an effect on me. It did. A sudden warmth began to spread down my abdominal area and thighs as I realized I wanted him. Wanted the warmth to continue.

I'm not ready for this, I thought. I'd been thinking about Byron and about the romance between Lianne and Kyle. I just had lovemaking on the brain. That's all it was. I wasn't even sure I liked Jason Foxx, much less desired him.

Before I could think of a smart remark to defuse the situation, he knelt beside me, put one arm around my shoulder and pulled me close.

He looked at me for what seemed like a full minute, yet I'm sure it took no longer than a microsecond. Then I felt his lips on mine, tentative at first, almost like a nibble that developed into a kiss full of passion and promise.

His moves took me by surprise, but I discovered I loved the way he kissed.

Get a grip, I told myself and fortunately my head took command of my body. I pulled my mouth away and shook my head. "I don't think—"

"Tell me you didn't enjoy it."

"I can't, but—"

"Look, Zoe, I know your situation, but we can work around it."

"It's not possible right now."

"Look, I know you're probably scared and maybe feel a little guilty, but you can't give up the rest of your life."

"I haven't. Someday I may even love again. But—how do I explain this? I still love Byron. And I'm not ready to be with anyone."

"No matter what happens, you're always going to love him." Jason slipped back into his shirt. "But you're a young woman and have needs and passions."

"Maybe so, but I'm not ready to make that irrevocable step away from him and my marriage."

"That's not being fair to yourself."

"Jason, we're missing an important step here," I said. "Even if Byron didn't exist, I'd want to go slowly. Maybe after we'd established a friendship maybe then I'd want more."

"So, what you're saying is you want to be friends?"

"Maybe, yes, I guess that's what I'm saying." For a moment, it felt strange telling him my feelings, but in the next moment, it felt entirely natural. "I'm just not a woman who jumps into bed with a man simply because she's horny. But I also want you to understand that we may never be more than friends. It's too early in the game, but I do know I'm not desperate."

He looked as if the thought had not occurred to him. "Okay. I can relate to that," he said. There were a few brief seconds of silence then he said, "Might even be fun."

"What?"

"Dating," he said.

"What a concept," I said. "And we thought of it all by ourselves."

He laughed. "All right, Zoe Barrow. How about dinner tomorrow night?"

I felt entirely comfortable with that idea and nodded.

"Decide where you want to go," he said. "And I'll pick you up about seven."

"Sounds like fun, Jason Foxx."

"See you tomorrow," he said and hopped back over the deck rail and into the darkness.

I kept thinking about him and the idea entered my head that I must be crazy. I probably should have gone ahead and jumped into bed with him—just acted without thinking about it. I'd certainly enjoyed the feel of his mouth on mine and the warmth of his body. I also knew I'd felt a stirring of emotions, which I thought were dead and buried. It was the first time I'd felt anything like desire for months.

I stood and picked up our empty beer cans and my afghan, turned and walked inside. The cats followed, tails at full staff.

Sex should never be analyzed, I told myself. It should be spontaneous and just enjoyed.

I closed up the apartment and headed for my cold, empty bed. That's when I realized there were tears on my cheeks.

I don't know if I heard a noise or dreamed it, but something woke me up and the cats, lying against the curve of my back, were on the alert—ears forward, listening. I listened too, and when I didn't hear anything else, drifted back into a fitful sleep.

Anthony Garcia chased after me in my dreams. Time and time again I eluded him, but he kept coming and each time he'd raise his gun to shoot me, I'd jerk myself partially awake. I'd go back to sleep and dream the same dream again.

Once, just before daylight, I got up, looked outside, checked all the doors and windows and after finding nothing wrong, crawled back into bed. This time, I slept without dreaming.

That short good rest got interrupted. Harry called shortly after six a.m. "Zoe, are you awake?" he asked.

"I am now."

"Damn it. It's bad news."

"What, Harry?"

"Mary Margaret Peppard was found in a motel, throat slashed. She's just off Airport Boulevard, Arrowhead Lodge."

"Mary Margaret? How?" My next thought was of Avery. "Peppard's still in Seton, isn't he?"

"Good question. I have no idea, but I'll find out." He paused and then asked, "What the hell is going on here?"

He couldn't see my shrug, but he wasn't really expecting an answer. "You want to meet me there?"

"Naw, I'll pick you up," he said. "Let's hope this turns out to be the break we need."

Early one morning a large pool of blood was found—giving the impression that some dark and dreadful tragedy had been enacted but nothing was ever learned concerning it. (Excerpted from: Austin History Center Records.)

Chapter 17

Harry gave me the known details as we sped north on Interstate 35 to Airport Boulevard. The night manager at Arrowhead Lodge had found a woman in bed naked and dead.

"Her throat was cut," Harry said. "Strange thing though, the patrol officer first on the scene didn't notice her neck right away. He was getting ready to call in a suicide."

"No way," I said.

"Well, he changed his mind right after he got a better look. A Texas driver's license found in the woman's purse matched the victim's general looks and description," he continued. "Official identification is still pending."

Arrowhead Lodge was made of dun-muckle-brown Austin native stone. Built in the late forties or fifties it was set several feet back from the road. No other buildings or houses were around it and the land on the backside was full of scrub cedar and mesquite trees. Seen in the pale light of dawn, it didn't look too bad, but I knew when the sun came up, the sleaze would show. A double arched drive-through led directly into an interior courtyard/parking area. Individual cabins, each connected to a one-car garage with pull-down doors, had been all the vogue when these old motels were built. The idea being, of course, your car would be protected and you'd have privacy. Small half-dead shrubs perched in front of each cabin.

"One thing about these old cabins," said Harry, "you didn't worry about your car getting get broken into or stolen."

"Or your wife seeing your car."

"Was that a sexist remark?" he asked.

"How about spouse? That works doesn't it?"

The motel, along with similar-style others around town, often made the top ten list around town as a hot bed of illegal activities; those garages made anonymity so easy.

Room 105 was a corner room on the northeast side of the one story structure and now bustled with city cops, a police photographer, fingerprint technicians, the medical examiner and a couple of deputy sheriffs. Normal rules at a homicide were the fewer people inside the roped-off crime-scene area the better. Harry would be the primary detective and as such would be allowed in without question. An exception was made for me, but only on Harry's say so.

Our first look told us the woman looked exactly like the photo we had of Mrs. Peppard and she actually did look as if she were only asleep.

"I can see why the officer thought it was suicide," I said as we walked inside, my hands behind my back. It took a few minutes to get my mind all set to view the body. No matter how many times I see violent death I never got used to it. And the odors that assault my senses, especially in such close quarters, made my insides churn.

The whole room reeked of blood and urine and feces, caused when death releases the muscles, and those were the strongest smells. Underlying all those were the cloying ancient smells of the motel room: smoke, sex, vomit, mold.

It took a lot to keep my stomach from erupting for the next three minutes. That's how long it took for the nerves in my nose to get numbed to the odors. It was a trick I'd learned at the Academy as a female officer who never wanted to lose her cookies in front of the guys, so I took the advice to heart. I learned to force myself to think of my favorite smells until the gag reflex calmed.

A strikingly pretty woman, who worked for the medical examiner, was kneeling by the bed. Her dark hair was tied back and emphasized the almond-shaped eyes of her Hispanic ancestry. She pulled the sheet back for Harry to get a closer look. "She didn't make it easy. There are multiple scratches and cuts on her hands like she tried to fight him off." She pointed a gloved finger at the woman's torso. "See her chest? He stabbed her twice. A near fatal one went into her heart but he made sure by slitting her throat."

By now I'd managed to turn off my emotions to the horror of what had happened here. Managed to forget that this was a human being who lived and breathed and now had died. Turn the victim into a clinical study for the time being. Later, I'd feel emotion, but not now. It was the only way to remain sane.

"Then he pulled the sheet up? That's a bit strange," said Harry, who stood beside the bed where Mary Margaret lay.

"Maybe he felt some remorse," I said and immediately thought of her husband. "And that means he knew her—probably intimately."

Harry glanced up. "Her face wasn't touched. She's much prettier than her picture." He turned to the medical examiner. "Any idea yet on a timeframe?"

"Sure." She frowned and stood. "Sometime in the last twenty-four hours. And if I had a better guess you *know* I'd tell you." She turned and smiled. "But ask me again tomorrow."

Harry moved out of the way as she came to where he'd been standing and leaned down to examine several blood spatters on the sheet and pillow.

"Most likely she was killed right here on the bed," she said. "If we're lucky, she bled on him and he had to shower. If so, we'll find hair samples and run a DNA."

Harry and I had moved over to the doorway out of her way. "Zoe," he said after a few moments. "Looks like I'll be here for a while. I'll have to make notes and a detailed sketch of the scene."

"Even with them taking pictures and videos?"

"The old-fashioned way works best for me. And we'll question the manager. Find out who rented the room and who visited her. What I hope," said Harry, "is to find a good witness and get the police artist to sketch a drawing of the killer."

"Harry, you're dreaming."

Harry looked over to where a young black man stood dusting the surface of a double dresser for prints and asked, "Got anything, Gerard?"

"Man, somebody did a real number on this room—wiped it clean. But I'll come up with partials, Harry. And he's bound to have missed someplace. That's about all I can tell you."

I knew Gerard Bell, an excellent evidence technician and fingerprint specialist. If there were anything, he'd find it. And if there was a print, it would go through AFIS, the Automated Fingerprint Identification System and maybe spit out a name. It wasn't going to be easy I thought, but sometimes you get lucky.

"The manager told the first patrol officer Mrs. Peppard wasn't the person who had rented the cabin. He wasn't sure what the guy looked like, and that he couldn't be expected to remember everyone who'd rented a room here." Harry smiled a thoroughly evil smile. "But he's holding back and I'll have to convince him it's in his own best interest to tell me everything."

On our way to the crime scene, Harry had discovered from dispatch that Peppard had been released from Seton Hospital this morning and should be at home.

In our town, the M.E. office has complete charge of a body and usually they notified the next of kin. They could, however, get APD to do it, so I wasn't too surprised when Harry asked.

"You want to inform Avery Peppard since you know him?"

"Not really, but I will."

"I know what you mean." He reached into his pocket for his keys. "Take my car and I'll get one of the patrols to take me back to headquarters."

"Wouldn't you rather I stay awhile and help you with the questioning?"

A young man with an ID pinned onto his plaid shirt walked in as I spoke and Harry said, "Here's my help now. Glad you could join us, dude."

That expression seemed out of character for Harry, but this was the first time I'd seen him with a younger male officer and I knew that's how some the younger ones talked.

Harry began filling in the other detective and I left.

The early rush hour traffic had thinned as I drove west on Koenig Lane, turned onto the Mo-Pac freeway and headed south for Westlake Hills and Peppard's house. It was shortly after ten a.m. when I arrived and rang the doorbell. Peppard looked much better than the last time I saw him. He greeted me with a look of surprise and I noticed he moved with the stiffness of someone who'd recently had surgery.

"Avery? May I come in?"

His face registered surprise, but he managed a wan smile and stood aside for me to enter. He closed the door and led the way to the living room, motioning for me to sit on a white leather sofa. "Zoe? What brings you—have you found out something about my wife?" A brief look of expectation changed as he realized that the news might not be good.

"I'm sorry, Avery," I said. "We found her, but she's . . ." I didn't have to say she'd been killed as he could tell from my expression.

"Oh, my God. Are you, uh, sure? Where is she?" He buried his face in his hands and his shoulders shook.

I left him alone, not wanting to embarrass him, and walked down to the kitchen where I found a coffeepot already set up, but not yet activated. I turned it on and rummaged through the drawers and cabinets until locating two coffee mugs and two spoons. It wasn't until the coffee aroma awoke my sense of smell that I realized my emotions had still been shut down from the scene at the motel. I should have comforted Avery more, I thought. How could I have been so callous?

I found a carton of half-and-half and a sugar bowl and placed them on the countertop next to the mugs. I walked to a bay window and watched as two young squirrels cavorted in a huge pecan tree.

I had just poured the coffee when Avery came in, made his way to the breakfast table and sat down. He looked to be in control of himself, for now, and when I put the coffee, sugar and milk in front of him, he managed a brief smile.

"Sorry," he said.

"Are you okay? I really am sorry, Avery." I patted his shoulder awkwardly and sat across from him. "This isn't going to be easy, but why don't I tell you what we know and then, if you have questions you can ask them."

"Okay. And thanks."

I added sugar and milk to my mug and sipped before I began reciting the facts, giving him only what he really needed to know. It would be easier to break things up in small doses as there was a lot for him to deal with in the next few hours.

"Who found her?"

"The manager said the maid went into the room to clean it."

"Why was she in this crummy motel?"

"We don't know. The investigation has just begun."

"My God. I just can't believe it. Are you sure it's Mary Margaret?"

I nodded. "Of course, you'll have to identify her later, but she *is* the woman whose photo is on the driver's license found in her purse. The license that says she's Mary Margaret Peppard of this address."

"I mean, this is so bizarre," he said. "Someone's been trying to kill me but Mary Margaret winds up dead. I feel like I'm in a nightmare and can't wake up." He put his head in his hands and in a moment I heard him sob. His shoulders shook.

I remembered similar feelings when Byron was shot. The worst part was the frustration and helplessness when you realized things were totally out of your control.

When he'd pulled himself together, I said, "Avery, I'm not going to lie to you. It's not going to get any better for a while—no matter what anyone says."

He looked at me as if to ask "what would you know?" then apparently remembered my husband. "Was it that Garcia guy? Was he Mary Margaret's lover?"

"I don't see how. He was in state prison until three weeks ago."

Tears filled his eyes. "I don't understand. She had over five hundred thousand dollars yesterday. Surely she gave most or part of it to her lover. Why would he kill her if she gave him the money?"

My mouth must have dropped to the floor. "She gave him what? How do you know? Why didn't you tell me?"

"I was too embarrassed," he said. "My bank president

called yesterday and said Mary Margaret had cleaned out several of our joint accounts—checking and savings. She only got eighty to ninety thousand from there. I asked my lawyer to check and when he called back he said she'd also cleaned out two money management accounts yesterday. The liquid ones that could be cashed without penalty."

I managed to close my mouth while he spoke. "And that netted how much? $500,000?" He nodded and his attitude about it seemed odd until I realized that this was only walking around money to him and not worthy of a mention.

And it served no purpose to tell him the money had probably signed Mary Margaret's death warrant. People have been killed for much less.

After a few minutes, I called some friends he mentioned to come stay with him and waited until they came. I used the waiting time to call my boss at work and tell him what time I'd be in and then made an appointment for Avery to go to the medical examiner's office to identify his wife. When the couple arrived I was able to take them aside and get their promise to go with Avery to the coroner.

I gave Avery a brief hug before I left. His eyes were red-rimmed, and he looked smaller now. He'd already been through enough with his own brush with death and losing his wife would have broken a lesser man. But he'd found his stiff businessman face, and I felt he'd take it all in stride, until the shock wore off, at least.

At my office, I went immediately into Lieutenant Hamilton's office to fill him in on what had happened.

"Harry Albright's already called to ask if I'd be willing to send you back to work with him," he asked. "Is that okay with you?"

"Thanks, Ham. I feel as if I've got to stay now."

"And this Peppard guy says his wife cleaned him out to the

tune of five hundred thousand dollars?"

"That's only chicken feed to him, but yes. That's what she got."

"No wonder she wound up dead."

"Exactly. I'm hoping we get a print, a hair or something from this guy—anything."

Hamilton told me to carry on and after I grabbed a cup of coffee, I checked telephone messages at my desk. Only one message was important enough to return—the one from Jason Foxx.

When I reached him, he said he'd heard already on the police radio.

"I had to be the one to tell Avery," I said.

"How did he take it?"

"Pretty bad," I said. "He was real shook at first, but he got it together. I think he'll be okay."

"Does this connect to Tami Louise and the guy who shot Peppard?"

"All I can say now is ask me another time, Jason. You know I can't detail an active investigation."

"Okay." He didn't press. "Look, the reason I called was to see if you still wanted to have dinner with me tonight."

"I don't know what time I'll be finished," I said and found myself feeling a little uncomfortable. On one hand, dinner with him didn't mean much, but on the other, it had all the earmarks of being a date and I wasn't sure about that. "I'm working with Harry."

He picked up on my hesitation and probably guessed what I was feeling. "Okay, but it's just dinner—no big deal. Why don't you call me later if it looks like you'll have some free time?"

I said okay and after we hung up, I walked over to the main building, sat at Harry's desk and looked for some logic in what had happened.

Had Mary Margaret's lover killed her because she gave him money? If money was his object all along, that amount was only the tip of the iceberg.

Harry showed up looking exhausted, and I knew how he felt. I'd had so little sleep last night that I was typing gibberish on the computer.

"Got anything?" I asked.

"Not yet. That night clerk's keeping his mouth shut," he said. "His lawyer came in before I could use what little leverage I had."

"So that's a dead end?"

"Until we get some lab results. We found lots of hairs in the shower and the room. Surely one belongs to our killer. Wonder if Garcia knew Tami Louise?" Harry asked, leaning back in his swivel-type chair. He put up his feet up, crossed his arms over his chest.

I was sitting opposite him across his desk. "If he did, what would that prove?"

"Probably nothing, but Tami and Avery knew each other. Tami dies, Avery gets shot by Garcia and Avery's wife is killed. What's the common denominator here?"

I knew he didn't expect an answer, so I didn't. I also didn't remind him how we thought Avery's shooter had been going for me.

"Something I learned a long time ago," he said, "about how tenuous connections usually hide more substantial ties. Especially when you're dealing with homicide. Both women had their throats cut. If the M.E. can determine the slashes are alike and that the same knife was used, we'll be cooking."

With that said, he dropped his arms and legs and scooted his chair until his legs were underneath the desk. "The connections all seem to be to Avery, not Garcia. But if Garcia knew Tami and killed her because she found out he planned to kill Avery, then hey, we're *really* getting somewhere."

"But who killed Mary Margaret? And why?"

"Had to be her lover," he said. "But if Garcia killed Tami—I should check to see if he ever used a knife."

"Too bad Tami's trick book got taken from us. I'd bet a month's pay the killer's name was in there."

He slowly began shifting folders, papers, notebooks and envelopes that were piled on his desk. "We'll just have to start again from scratch, Zoe."

"Okay." I took the yellow legal pad he offered and picked up a pen. "What do we know for sure? Avery Peppard came to me with his tale of a hit man hired by his wife and her lover who may possibly be a cop. Two weeks later Tami Louise was killed. Why?"

"A disgruntled customer?" He ticked them off. "A random sexual assault or she saw something she shouldn't have."

"We can't rule out Anthony Garcia, although we have no proof he was anywhere near. A good hit man wouldn't be seen," I said. "If he was hired to take out Peppard, he could have been hired to take out Tami for some reason. Next, we have two other males on the scene who either saw or talked to her just prior to her death. Kyle Raines and Avery Peppard."

"Agreed. I'd bet money Hebron talked to her, too. I doubt she could get into that empty room without his say-so. And don't forget Jason Foxx," he reminded me. "He's really not lived in Austin long enough to have known Mary Margaret, but by some stretch, he could be her lover."

I didn't want to think about Jason Foxx being involved with Mary Margaret Peppard. "And let's not forget our small time hood and local pimp, Stevie Crooks, either."

"Stevie? I don't think so," said Harry. "Sure he knew Tami, but I doubt he knew the Peppards. And he's not the

194

lover boy type anyway."

"Well, *I* don't think Jason or Kyle had anything to do with it, but we do suspect everyone, don't we?"

"If Garcia was after you and not Peppard, that may be all he's guilty of and that takes him out of the Tami Smuts and Mary Margaret Peppard equation."

"I agree."

"Okay, what happened after Tami died and how does it connect, if it does? Tami's trick book was snatched, and you and Lianne were assaulted."

"Next," I said, "Avery says a man with a knife came after him, yet shortly after that someone, most likely Garcia, shot him. Although I may have been the target instead of Peppard. And Tami and Mary Margaret were both killed with a knife. Has the report come in yet on what type of knife was used on Tami Louise?"

He shrugged. The phone on his desk rang, but before he picked up, he said, "I've got an idea I want to check out on Garcia's arrest records— "Albright here. Yeah, Gerard." He began writing on a telephone notepad. "Okay, fine. Call me when you have more." He hung up and told me the finger-print specialist thought he might have something for us later today on a partial thumbprint.

"Great." I rubbed my gritty eyes and wondered if I could find any coffee that hadn't been brewed in Homicide's cof-feepot. The stuff that came out of there would grow hair on Mr. Clean. If not, I'd walk over to my office. One thing my unit prided itself on was good coffee.

I got to the door and Harry called out, "Zoe? What's this?"

I turned and looked. He was holding an envelope out and I walked back to his desk. The police photo lab envelope had my name on it.

"That must be the film I found in Tami's apartment—"

My voice trailed off when I realized the possibilities. I grabbed the envelope out of his hand, slid my fingers under the sealed flap, opened it and quickly fanned through the pictures.

The color photos were of Tami and several different men in various stages of nudity and near nudity. Some of the men were totally unrecognizable but there were a couple of big surprises.

It was like getting six numbers in the Texas Lotto game. Like five sevens coming up on a slot machine in Las Vegas or Reno. Lights flashed and bells rang.

Police Chief Boss Thorp revealed he knew the identity of the killer who shot a farmer and his wife and tortured their 25-year-old daughter with lit cigarettes before shooting her, but was unable to prove it in court. Ballistics was a new science and bullets were sent to NY to an expert who said the murder weapon was a Spanish-made pistol. Thorp went to his grave in 1975 without naming the person he suspected. (Compiled from: Austin History Center Records.)

Chapter 18

Harry glanced at the photo, leaned forward, then his feet stomped hard on the floor. "My God," he said. "Will you look at that sanctimonious old fart. I was in Academy with him and he always thought he was better than anybody else."

The picture he held was a clear shot of the fatherly image of Lieutenant Andrew Nichols of Internal Affairs. The same Andrew Nichols who'd led my questioning sessions. He sure didn't look like anyone's father in this picture. Totally nude, he lay on the bed with a naked Tami beside him and she leaned over his chest with her hand on his abdomen. You couldn't mistake his erection flapping in the breeze.

"Man, it's a cinch these weren't posed," I said. "Who took them? And why weren't they ever developed?"

"Nichols will be ruined," said Harry, ignoring my questions. His voice sounded gleeful, but his expression told me nothing. "That jackass. And he had the nerve to accuse me—" He stopped abruptly.

"Would he kill someone to keep these pictures a secret?" I asked, ignoring what he'd almost said. I'd ask him about that later.

I looked at the remaining pictures and got a jolt when I recognized Kyle Raines with Tami Louise. My teammate wore a pair of Levi's and no shirt and Tami had on a see-through pale green nightgown.

Damn you Kyle, I thought, and handed the snapshot to Harry. "This guy works with me. He's married and has a rep as a womanizer."

"Could that picture cause him trouble?"

"Maybe with his wife, and I doubt the brass would be pleased. Morals code or something. But murder? I don't think he's capable of cold-blooded killing. Not if—"

"Zoe, *anyone* is capable of murder given the right provocation and circumstances." Harry leaned back in his chair again. "But the killer must not have known about these." He tapped the picture in his hand. "Otherwise he would gone for the film when he got her trick book."

"The undeveloped rolls just lay loose in her dresser, not hidden or anything. Knowing Tami, maybe she thought she could extort a little money."

"Most likely they were for bargaining," he said. "If she had a compromising picture with a cop who'd want to hassle her? Or if she got into trouble with the narcs, she could make a bargain using them."

I looked at the final two photos. Both were fuzzy, and a little out of focus, but you couldn't mistake Tami sitting beside a man. Their location was the cabin of a boat. The photographer must have had a telephoto lens. Tami had on a green and black print bikini bottom and nothing on top, while the man wore an open plaid shirt over dark swim trunks.

One of Tami's legs lay across the man's lap and he sat sideways caressing her bare left breast with his hand. You could tell she was laughing. The upper portion of his face was in shadow and more profile than full-face. He wore a cowboy hat, dark sunglasses and his nose hooked on the end.

The two pictures had been taken one right after the other, with both Tami and the man barely moving between takes, and he only slightly clearer in the second than in the first. It looked like he tried to deliberately keep from being recognized. Did he know about the photos?

Despite his effort to remain incognito, he looked vaguely familiar. I knew him from somewhere. That hooked nose was unmistakable. I'd seen a nose like that recently, but where?

I sifted faces through my mind and came up with a possible. "Whoa!" I said aloud. Could I be imagining it? "Who does this look like, Harry?" I asked and handed the photos over.

He studied the prints, placing them side by side on his desk and then grunted, opened his desk drawer, and pulled out the biggest magnifying glass I'd ever seen.

"You've got to be kidding," I said.

"What?" he asked without looking up.

"You and your glass, Sherlock. Where in the world did you get that thing?"

He didn't answer for a full twenty seconds. "It came with my Hardy Boys Junior Detective Club Kit."

"Your what?"

"Sheesh. You're either too young or too female."

"Forget I asked. Just tell me, who is he?"

He scrutinized both pictures through the glass again. "I'd like to see a blow-up and I wouldn't want to swear in court—"

"Harree, say it. Say, it's who I think—"

"—but I think it's that security guy over at the Texas Star, Richard Hebron."

"All riiight." I could hardly contain my excitement. "Let's get the lab to see if they can do better. Focus on his face."

Harry leaned back in his chair and looked at the ceiling for a time. "Wait, I know this guy named Randy." He rocked back a little more, and looked at me with narrowed eyes. "Enlargement might distort or washout the details too much. But if anyone can pull if off, Randy can."

I looked at one of the photos of the man again, using Harry's glass. "Harry, I'd bet a month's pay it's him. And he said maybe he'd seen her once or twice, but she wasn't a regular at the hotel and he'd actually never met her." I picked up the other photo. I felt a tingle in my abdominal area—that feeling you get when you know your case is on the right track.

"I know it's him," I said. "If we can prove it's Hebron and if we get a fingerprint or some DNA hair samples from Tami's room, we can make a case here. I know that's a whole bunch of ifs."

Harry tapped out a number on his phone and seconds later said, "Randy? Albright here. What's up?" Harry leaned back and laughed. "Oh, yeah, same old, same old. Yeah, I know. Look, man, I've got a photo and I need a quick miracle." He listened briefly before continuing his persuasion.

"I know I still owe you, Randy," said Harry. "Okay, but that's bullshit. This one is absolutely, positively priority. Two steak dinners and two bottles of Scotch up front? Right, the good stuff? That's highway robbery." He glanced at his watch. "Within the hour. Okay, thanks, Randy."

Harry slid the two pictures into his inside jacket pocket. "Grab your coat and hat, Zoe. We're heading to south Austin to see the best photo specialist I know. Randy's got computer equipment that does everything but talk to you."

"In the meantime, what do we do with these?" I held up the rest of the photos.

"Lock them up in the evidence safe." I placed the snapshots back inside the envelope and put them into a plastic bag. He wrote the date, initialed it and we took them down to the basement where evidence is checked in and stored.

"Didn't the Medical Examiner say he might match the knife?"

Harry only grunted.

On the way to Harry's car I said, "We need to check on the other men we recognize."

"Damn straight. And I personally intend to check on Nichols."

We reached his car, but I didn't get in just yet. I stood leaning against the fender. "What's the deal on Nichols?" I asked. "If you want to tell me, that is."

Harry stood beside me, putting his rear end against the fender also. We both faced out. "It's a long story," he said.

"Can you give me the short version?"

"Three years ago, my wife was dying from an inoperable brain tumor. One night I got plastered and ran into this woman I knew—a hooker who had been my C.I. for about three months."

I thought he might give me more information than I wanted to know. "Okay, I get the picture. What does that have to do with anything?" Knowing about his wife's illness did give me a new perspective on the man and knowing he'd finally gone to a hooker only made him more human to me.

"Nichols saw me and threatened to tell my wife if I didn't report it to my lieutenant."

"Okay, so he's a jackass, but if Tami wasn't blackmailing him what possible motive could he have for killing her?" I glanced at Harry but couldn't tell what he was thinking.

"Maybe she *was* blackmailing him."

"I remember the last time I saw her. She was frightened of someone. And how," I asked, "does Tami's death connect to Mary Margaret being killed?"

"Believe me, there *is* one, we just have to find it." He pushed himself away from the car, walked around and un-locked the door. "You just going to stand there or what?" He was fumbling to put the key into the ignition.

"You don't need me out at your buddy's," I said. "I think I'll go talk to Lianne."

He snapped his head around to look at me. "What does she know about anything?"

"She's doing the nasty with Kyle Raines or getting ready to at least."

"The hell she is. Didn't you say he was married?"

"Yes."

"Oh hell. Doesn't she know any bet . . ." He let his voice trail off, turned the key and revved the engine when it caught. "Well, it's not my business."

"I know. Mine either. Go see what can be done with those pictures and I'll go see what our friend knows about her current love interest."

"Okay, but damn her to hell and back. She should know better." He put his car in gear and took off like the maniacal driver he was.

I got in my car and used the cellular to call up to vice for Lianne. They said she was home because she was pulling duty tonight. Which meant she was probably sleeping. I called and got her answering machine. "Come over for dinner," I said. "I know you're working tonight, but be there around six or so. I'm making my world famous chili."

Thinking about Lianne and Kyle boggled my mind. Not just that Kyle had messed around with Tami but was he involved in her death? I dislike that macho part of Kyle who thinks he's irresistible, but aside from that he's basically a good guy. He wouldn't kill anyone, would he?

Richard Hebron was a more likely candidate. But to overlook Kyle as a suspect was to have blinders on. Kyle was there the night Tami died. Peppard's wife was involved with a cop. Kyle is a cop and a womanizer.

Kyle and Mary Margaret. An assumption that Tami Louise and Mary Margaret knew each other. Could Kyle be that connection?

That scenario was almost too far-fetched and it called for some real stretches, but I needed to wander down that lane for a little time anyway.

I fed the cats, showered and started making the chili, trying to decide the best way to approach my friend. It wasn't going to be easy. I didn't want to jump on her immediately.

As it turned out, my worrying about what to say didn't matter. The minute she walked in, I knew she had a chip on her shoulder.

"I only came tonight," she said in a tone only slightly warmer than an iceberg, "because I think it's time you and I aired our feelings about Kyle and me."

"Lianne, it's really none of my business who you date."

"Then what?"

I told her about the photograph.

"So? Kyle once knew Tami intimately," she said. "Big deal. It was a long time ago, I'm quite sure."

"Don't you see that puts him high on our suspect list?"

"Suspect list? You suspect Kyle? That's the most ridiculous thing I've ever heard."

"I think so, too. But I have to look at the facts," I said. "He was at the hotel the night she was killed—"

"On duty and supposed to be there. You know that."

"He was probably one of the last people to see her alive, and he fits the description of the person seen near her room shortly before her body was found."

"I can't believe what I'm hearing. You've worked with Kyle for years!" Her tone became more defensive by the minute. "How can you even begin to suspect him?"

"Lianne, think about it. Worst case—Kyle somehow got involved with Mary Margaret Peppard. Tami found out about it, threatened to expose her relationship with him. Or maybe Tami thought she could blackmail Mrs. Peppard."

She put her hands over her ears. "I'm not going to listen to this. You're jealous because I've found someone, and you can't stand it because I'm sleeping with him and you're—"

"Lianne, this has nothing to do with you and Kyle as a couple. It has everything to do—"

"Oh, damn. I've never known you to be jealous before, but maybe being without sex for so long is finally getting to you. Kyle said the same thing the other night and dumb me—I defended you."

"My lack of sex is not the issue here."

"Then just what is?" she asked.

I hated what I was going to say, but I had to find out if she knew anything. Like, did she know where Kyle was last night when Mrs. Peppard was murdered? If she could alibi him that would go a long way to putting Kyle totally out of the picture. "Okay, just tell me one thing. Was Kyle with you last night?"

She jumped up and walked to the door. "This stupid conversation is at an end. You want to know if Kyle was with me? You want me to alibi him? I am not believing this." She opened the door and paused. "I hope, because we have too many years of friendship to throw away, that you'll come to your senses, and soon. Kyle's not a killer and you can just shove that idea up your behind and sit on it!"

She slammed out.

"Who does she think she is?" I asked Melody and Lyric. They came into the living room, wanting attention, but I was still too angry, and petted too rough and they took off, highly incensed.

And where does she get off bringing up my sex life or my lack of one? She knew better. And she knew if Kyle held back information about a relationship with Tami it could look bad. He knew it, too. What was he thinking?

I slammed around the apartment, complaining loudly about the unfairness of life and the hypocrisy of friends. I grabbed a broom and stormed outside and began sweeping the deck. Lianne just didn't know what she was getting into with Kyle. Nothing but heartbreak.

My pager chirped. I stomped inside and read the phone number on the screen. Not familiar, but I dialed the number anyway as I trooped back outside.

His voice was barely above a whisper, and he called me several choice names beginning with "bitch" and ending with "whore." He said I deserved to die for what I did to Jesse. He said I'd pay dearly. I slammed down the receiver.

Anthony Garcia blamed me? My husband is just a shell lying in a nursing home all because of his precious Jesse Garcia. My whole life has changed because of his stinking nephew. Then Anthony tried to kill me and put Avery Peppard in the hospital. But he blames me? "Get real, you scum-bag!"

I finished sweeping the porch. My tirade about crazy people now included Garcia. However, Garcia I could attribute to just being a total jerk-off. Fuming about my pal was something else.

For a little while I wallowed in anger and even enjoyed the feeling until I realized I was more angry with myself than with Lianne. Deep in my gut, I didn't want to think Kyle was a killer. Lianne obviously cared for him, and accusing him was the worst thing I could do.

How could I? And Lianne meant much too much to me. During those long hours when Byron was so bad, she'd kept my chin up when I didn't have the energy to hold it up myself. She'd listened to my worries about the hospital and doctors. Anytime I needed her day, or night, all I had to do was pick up the phone and she'd come over and stay with me.

I'd been a total idiot and I knew it. I picked up the telephone to call then realized she was probably on her way to work. I'd call later. I put the phone down but it rang again immediately.

I growled "hello" into the receiver.

It was Harry. "Zoe, are you okay?"

"A few minutes ago I had a telephone threat from Garcia."

"Did you report it?"

"No way. I can't deal with all that paperwork tonight."

"He called you? How'd he get your number?"

"No, no. He paged me. I called him back, thinking it was one of my informants."

"Did you at least put the caller ID blocker on when you called him back?"

I thought for a moment. "Yeah, I guess so . . . hell, I don't know. I, uh, always do when I call a C.I." I wouldn't swear to anything, but I didn't want to explain to him how I'd accused my best friend's lover of being a murderer, and so I changed the subject. "What's going on?"

Melody came and jumped into my lap, which is totally unlike her usual standoffish persona, and Lyric lay atop my foot. They were trying to make up for running off before, even though it had been all my fault. I rubbed Melody under the chin and waited for Harry to say why he'd called.

"My photographer friend called, said the pics turned out good. I drove all the way out to Oak Hill, but he wasn't home. Left a note on his door that some emergency came up and for me to come back tomorrow early."

"Well, at least he's got something for us."

Harry grunted and told me he'd also done some checking on Andrew Nichols, the I.A. man with Tami. "I pulled a copy of his fingerprints and ran them through the AFIS in connection with both murder scenes."

"And?"

"Got caught and got my ass chewed by Lieutenant Olivera. And I was told in no uncertain terms to back off entirely."

"I'm sorry, Harry." Melody suddenly dug her claws into my leg and jumped from my lap. "Ouch."

"You talking to me?"

"No. One of my cats. So, you're going to forget about Nichols?"

"No way. I'm finding out what he's been up to—that arrogant bastard needs to be taken down a peg."

"Are we a little hostile here?"

"Damn straight." He grunted and added, "You might feel hostile too, after what I heard about you."

"About me?"

"Uh-hummm. Nichols tried to spread a rumor around that you killed Jesse Garcia for revenge."

"I knew he thought it; I could tell by the way he acted when he questioned me, but it's not true, Harry." I felt my stomach churn at hearing how easily Nichols could have ruined me.

"Hell, I know that. But you were cleared and someone up on the fifth floor warned Nichols to watch his mouth."

"Why would Nichols start such a rumor? The evidence showed it wasn't true."

"He hates female cops," he said. "Thinks the force has been diluted by hiring females and minorities. He goes out of his way to give minorities a hard time."

"And that's his only reason?"

"Yeah."

"Anyone that prejudiced and suspicious shouldn't have the job he does. How did he get in I.A. with that attitude?"

"He knew the right butt to kiss." Papers rustled over the line and Harry said, "Zoe, I've known him for a long time, and believe me, he's an egomaniac of the first order."

"Harry, maybe he was involved with Tami's death, but can you see him with Mary Margaret Peppard? Think about it."

"That scenario plays for me. Money and power are two things he craves," he said. "He could have met them socially and saw an opportunity. The Peppard millions would give Nichols all he desires."

"You just think about how much trouble you'll be stepping in if you go for him after you've been warned."

"Sounds like you might care what happens to me."

"No. I'd just hate having to do all the damn paperwork."

Originally, Pflugerville was settled by a farmer from Germany named Henry Pfluger. He brought his large family to live there in 1853. Soon other settlers came and the little town grew. Pflugerville naturally has its own police force. (Excerpted from: Austin History Center Records.)

Chapter 19

Fifteen miles north of downtown Austin, and a mile or so east of Interstate 35, is the town of Pflugerville. The town stayed a small farming community until the mid-1980s when Pflugerville suddenly became a bedroom community for Austin. Taxes and the crime rate were lower, schools were smaller, more able to deal with young people on a one-on-one basis, and the commute to downtown Austin was a leisurely twenty minutes on the interstate.

The nineties changed the quiet bedroom community once again. Dell Computer moved its major campus to Round Rock, just north of Pflugerville and Samsung moved its campus and headquarters to Pflugerville's southern edge. Suddenly the town grew to fifteen or twenty thousand in population. The town recently opened a million-and-a-half-dollar public library and kept trying to hold on to its close-knit community of eight to nine hundred folks from 1980.

Richard Hebron had a Pflugerville address, 1929 Palomino Lane. I had no idea where that was but I'd find it. I had questions I wanted answers to, and although I wasn't sure which ones to ask or which way to ask them, a talk with this man rated high on my list. With its own city police force, Pflugerville is out of APD's jurisdiction, meaning I'd better not step on anyone's official toes. I didn't mention my plan to Harry. Any toes that got mashed, it was my butt.

Twenty-five minutes later I drove into downtown Pflugerville and stopped at a gas station to ask directions. Palomino was north and east of downtown, and no more than eight blocks away. As I drove to the location, I admired the older homes along the way. Many were the well-preserved, lovely old two-story houses built fifty or sixty years ago with large front porches shaded by huge magnolia and pecan trees. After about six blocks, these homes abruptly ended and new housing additions had been tacked onto and around the older neighborhoods like knotty-pine trim added to ceilings of paneled oak. Palomino Lane had another housing style, which looked totally out of place next door to the new, hundred-thousand-dollar homes.

Not exactly a trailer park, but a whole neighborhood of trailers, some single and some double-wides. Many owners worked hard to make their lot attractive, planting grass and shrubs, hanging baskets with flowers; I even saw a picket fence or two. One place had a charming white gazebo with an old-fashioned porch swing in it.

Two blocks over on Palomino, a different story emerged. Trailers in dire need of maintenance and yards in desperate need of a cleanup. A two-toned, sun-faded pale blue 1954 Chevrolet, with rusting eyeball headlights looking ready to fall out, sat in one yard. At another, half the insides—the battery and what looked like a water pump—lay scattered a foot or so out into the street.

I found the correct number handwritten on the mailbox at Hebron's trailer. The place looked abandoned. The trailer, a single, was baby-turd brown. Paint peeled and rust spots trailed the bottom window frames holding scummy glass. Weeds choked what little grass grew in the yard. The driveway, two ruts really, was empty. I walked to the door and knocked.

As I expected, no one answered. I went to the corner and looked into the backyard. Waist-high weeds began three feet beyond the back of the trailer and continued up to some small scrub cedar trees. A few cinder blocks were scattered and a wooden fence ran across the back of the whole row of lots. On the other side of the fence stood a sparkling new housing addition. Was the developer of the new addition trying to hide things that might distract from his pristine project?

Back to my car, I looked across the street at the neighboring trailers. No one moved about despite the great weather. I climbed back into my car and rolled slowly down the street.

Two little boys on bicycles suddenly rounded the corner, turned again and began chasing each other around the intersecting cul-de-sac. I eased the car in their direction and stopped. "Do you know the man who lives in that brown trailer?" I asked as they rode slowly by me.

The older child just looked at me and kept riding. The younger one shook his head. I waited until they came around again. "Have you seen him? Yesterday or today?" The younger one said "No," and the older one stopped his bike and yelled at me over his shoulder. "We don't know him and we ain't suppose to talk to strangers. Come on, Billy."

Billy stopped his bike near my front fender, placing his hand on my car to keep balanced. He looked at me. "He's a mean old fart in his black hat. He wouldn't give me back my football when it went in his backyard." Billy rode off and this time they turned and rode in the opposite direction.

Back in Austin, I went directly to the Texas Star hotel. The students working in security were the same Twiddle-Dee and Twiddle-Dum that we'd interviewed the night Tami died. When I asked for Richard Hebron, they looked at me as if I'd asked which way was up—they only knew the language of down. After staring off into space for what seemed like half a day, one said the chief wasn't there and the other admitted they didn't know when Hebron would return. In unison, finally, they said the assistant night manager might know. But after thinking for eons, neither could remember who held that position, but swore someone at the front desk could tell me.

Are university students getting dumber or am I getting old? I stopped at the front desk and was escorted to an office behind the reception area.

The night manager, Dawnna Carter, was a striking black woman with reddish brown ringlets worn close to her skull. Her pale blue suit and white blouse spoke of her power position. "You're with the police?" Her tone was icy as she asked. I sat down while she looked at my badge again as if it might have changed in the few seconds she'd held it.

"Yes, ma'am, and I need to speak with your security chief, Richard Hebron. This is urgent police business."

She rose from the desk, ambled over and poked her head into the office next door, speaking to someone inside. "Do we have somebody in security here named Richard Hebron?"

I couldn't hear the answer and Ms. Carter slid around the doorjamb and inside the room where, hopefully, someone knew my quarry.

I waited patiently until she came back and watched until she'd put the plastic smile back on her face. "I'm sorry, Ms. Barrow. It's only my second day here and I'm a little unclear on hotel policy."

After being so frosty earlier, she'd finally showed a human side. "I understand. I'm sure you wouldn't want to do anything against the rules."

Soon a young woman came in handing a file folder to Ms. Carter and left without saying a word. The neophyte manager opened the folder and read it silently, moving her lips as she did so. "Mr. Hebron is on vacation and not due back for several days." She closed the folder and placed it on her desk. That was that. Her tone and actions implied; she'd done her duty.

"All right. Do you have an emergency address or telephone number where he can be reached?" Vacation? Hebron's abandoned trailer looked more like he'd flown the coop.

"I'm sorry." She wouldn't meet my eyes. "We don't monitor our employee's vacations."

"I see. May I have your supervisor's name, please?"

"You can call him, but I don't think—" She opened the folder again, looked for a second or two and then closed it. "A notation in red ink states Mr. Hebron will be in Mexico City for a few days."

Mexico City. A place where a man could get completely lost. And Tony Garcia and his friend had tried to use Mrs. Peppard's tickets to Mexico City. Did this prove Hebron was Mrs. P's lover? "Do you have a telephone number where Mr. Hebron is staying in Mexico?"

"I'm sorry. That's against company rules to give out employee phone numbers."

"Thank you, Ms. Carter. You've been most helpful." I stood to leave, giving her my card and asking her to telephone if she thought of anything else.

She opened the folder, smiled and slowly deliberated on where to place it. Even upside down I was able to read the words *El Grande Hotel.* "Muchas gracias, Ms. Carter."

Back at my unit, Lieutenant Hamilton and two of my team greeted me as they went out the door. Kyle Raines wouldn't even look at me. Ham smiled grimly and said they were on the way to serve a warrant and that he'd see me later.

I tried to catch Kyle's attention, but he pointedly ignored me. Couldn't blame him, I thought, it wasn't going to be easy to make amends with him or Lianne.

I contacted the El Grande in Mexico City. No, Mr. Hebron had not checked in yet, although he was due two days ago. And no, they hadn't heard from him.

What about Mary Margaret Peppard? Yes, they said, Mrs. Peppard also had a reservation, but she also had not checked in and they were still holding her room because it had been prepaid for a week. "Was Mr. Hebron's room prepaid also?" It had been, the clerk assured me. By Mrs. Peppard's credit card, the clerk said.

I got all excited—a tangible traceable proof of a link between Mary Margaret Peppard and Richard Hebron. I asked for a fax copy to be sent to me. He'd already given me the same information verbally, and for some reason he hesitated but finally agreed.

The plan probably was for Mary Margaret to stick with normal travel routines so she would present the presumption of innocence while her husband was blown away. But she'd made a mistake with charging rooms to their credit cards. A quick call to Peppard confirmed the Peppards usually stayed in the El Grande. Peppard wanted to talk but I cut him off.

I tried to reach Harry, but he wasn't at his office and no one knew where he was. I left a message in homicide for him to call. I also dialed his pager and punched in my phone number. "Where in hell are you, Harry?" I muttered. I felt excitement flipping butterfly wings in my stomach and I wanted to discuss things with him. Get his expert opinion. See if he agreed with me that this case was coming to a head.

Did Hebron or Garcia kill Mary Margaret? Which one and why? I'd vote on Garcia, but thought Hebron had hired him. Hebron was after her money.

Or maybe Hebron did it because Garcia screwed the job with Avery. Had Hebron already left for Mexico City? I made a note to check the airlines.

But how did Tami Louise's death fit in? Time to go at this from another angle, I thought, pushing the "ON" button for my computer. I tapped into the state law enforcement files and asked for information on one Richard Hebron. The first file didn't contain much more than what I already knew, but I kept pushing buttons until the screen filled with arrest reports during the three years he was at the sheriff's department. I printed up the reports.

One item immediately caught my eye. Ten months ago, Hebron had arrested Tami Louise Smuts. Then I realized, so what? All it proved was he had arrested the young woman. Just like the photo of Tami and Hebron, it only proved he'd spent some time with her. It reinforced the idea he'd lied about knowing her, but nothing else. No conspiracy or anything obvious like that.

I kept paging through the files and finally found another tidbit. Twenty months ago, Hebron arrested Anthony Garcia for serious bodily injury to a hooker. Two earlier arrests also listed Hebron as the arresting officer. But on the last one, Hebron had testified against Garcia, and his testimony helped send Garcia to Huntsville.

Then I got an unexpected bonus. Hebron had signed that arrest report as "Cowboy" Hebron. The Stetson he wore in the photo with Tami had been his undoing. And I was sure I remembered that name from Tami's trick book.

I needed Harry to bounce theories off of; he was the expert here. I tried to call him again, but he still wasn't in his office and he hadn't called in for messages either.

I also put in a request under Harry's name for Hebron's prints to be compared with the ones found at both women's murder scenes.

I left the office, spent a quiet evening at home and went to bed early, all the while wondering why Harry didn't contact me.

The telephone rang. My eyes felt as if I'd only just closed them but the big red numbers on the clock read one a.m. I grumbled and picked up the receiver.

"Zoe Barrow?"

When I answered yes, his words sent shivers down my spine. "If you wanna see Harry Albright alive, do exactly as I say."

"Okay. What?" Harry? I had not been able to reach him all evening. But it wasn't Harry.

"Get your ass out here."

"Out where?" I asked. Suddenly I recognized the voice. "Anthony?" Anthony Garcia.

"You need to come watch the show. I want you to see and feel his pain." He laughed. "After I do old Harry, then I'm gonna do your old man. Nice and slow. You'll pay for killing Jesse, bitch."

"Where are you?" I asked.

"I believe that sign outside says Pecan Groves Nursing Home." He laughed again. "Come alone. Unnerstand? I've got old Harry's radio. The minute I hear sumbody say cops's coming, I start slicing. You got thirty minutes."

The nursing home. God, he was at the nursing home.

He broke the connection before I could ask any more questions.

Garcia said he'd start slicing if I didn't come alone, and I believed him.

Don't let me be too late. I slid into the car. The ignition ground and I muttered, "Please, please, please start."

The engine caught. A minor fender-bender on the feeder road lured a virtual parade of gawkers. I fumed. I longed for a siren or a bubble light, but undercover cars don't carry such useful police stuff. Finally, I maneuvered around, jammed the gas pedal to the floorboard, and the Chrysler horsepower kicked in, pushing the speed to fifty-five, sixty, sixty-five.

If I don't get there in time, what will he do? Would he just start slashing, stabbing, killing?

A knife slicing the throat was silent; so final.

This damn traffic, why weren't these people home in bed? I found myself wishing Harry was driving. How in hell did he get caught anyway?

Traffic thinned a bit as I flew past the airport exit and I pushed the speed up to seventy, then eighty. What would I say if some diligent motorcycle officer stopped me for speeding?

I desperately needed help. But how? Since Garcia had Harry's radio, he'd very effectively cut me off. Even if I switched to a tactical channel, he'd switch too and listen.

No, it was too dangerous. If I called for backup, and dispatch put a call on the radio, he'd kill Harry and Byron for sure. I'd have to handle the situation alone.

I picked up my cell phone and dialed the nursing home. Maybe someone there knew what was going on. It rang and rang, but no one answered.

An icy cold chilled my veins.

Someone had cut the phone lines.

Fear had numbed my thinking process, but suddenly I realized who could help. If I could reach him. I grabbed the phone again and punched in Jason Foxx's number. When he answered I blurted out the situation.

"I'll be there in ten minutes," he said. "Don't go inside without me. I'm leaving now and I'll call you back from the car."

"I can't wait—I've only got thirty minutes."

"I'll be there in five," he said. "You wait." He broke the connection.

In 1861, in the midst of a grove of oaks and elms . . . north of the state capitol and seat of government, sat a gray limestone building . . . (Excerpted from: Austin History Center Records.)

Chapter 20

I parked, forcing myself to take some deep breaths. More than anything I wanted to rush inside and scream at Garcia—shoot him in the balls or something equally bad. But that would never work. This was not a one-person job; I didn't want Byron or Harry hurt. Just before I reached Pecan Groves, Jason had called and given his ETA. Two minutes, he said. So where in the hell was he?

My hand automatically reached into my pack for my gun. I removed the clip, checked it, and slid it back into place putting it on the bucket seat next to me. I pushed my seat as far back as it would go, reached down to untie, tighten, and retie my shoelaces.

I looked at my watch. Garcia had given me thirty minutes and time was nearly up; two lives depended on thirty short minutes.

How did Harry get caught in this deadly game? Damn you—you just had to get out there and wing this alone, didn't you, Harry? Why didn't you call me?

I couldn't wait any longer for Jason. I unlocked the car door, opened it and got out. Garcia had to be stopped now, even if it meant doing it alone.

Jason's tires squealed as he turned into the parking lot, and pulled to a halt in the empty space on the other side of my car. A little more than a minute had passed since his phone call but it felt like an hour.

I let out the breath I'd been holding. "Thanks for coming."

"No problem," he said.

I opened my car trunk and took out a Kevlar vest and a windbreaker which had Police written on it in big white letters. I pulled on the vest and jacket and then noticed he, too, had on a bulletproof vest.

"I bought it myself," he said to my unanswered question. "About six months before I got shot. No, I wasn't wearing it that night."

"You armed?" I asked as I checked my gun again. He nodded.

"Am I deputized or something?"

"You are in my book. I don't even want to think about the legalities of having you involved. Actually I don't give a damn right now. Not when my partner and my husband are in danger."

"I'll try to shoot only bad guys."

I looked at him; he wasn't trying to be funny. I gave him Garcia's description and the exact location of Byron's room. We headed inside the front door in a tactical formation—I led and he covered the rear. I made sure my position was clear and covered him as he moved closer. Just like in the movies.

The lobby and reception desk areas yawned emptily. A slight and muffled commotion came from Nursing One-West, the wing opposite the one which housed Byron. The noise stopped almost immediately.

A pine-scented cleaning smell assaulted my nostrils as I moved quickly to the opening of Byron's corridor, Nursing Two-East. I didn't enter but stood with my back against the wall beside the double-doorway entrance and listened. For a brief moment I thought I'd suddenly gone deaf, the silence was so complete. Gradually I became aware of faint murmurs from a TV located in someone's room.

I wondered about the nursing staff. The late, late shift is always a skeleton crew but were they all dead or just in hiding?

Jason held his position near the front door, semi-crouched next to a wing-backed visitor's chair. His eyes scanned, constantly alert for danger coming from any direction, but especially from Two-East. I chanced a quick peek down towards Byron's room. Emptiness stared back at me.

The hallways are fifteen feet wide. You could see and be seen the whole length if you entered. No cover or protection. But who'd ever expect to need cover in a nursing home?

I motioned for Jason to move up, and when he reached my side, I whispered, "We'd be totally exposed going down there—sitting ducks." I could feel an iciness forming in the exact center of my abdomen. Damn, I couldn't let fear gain an icy foothold anywhere. If I wanted to help Byron and Harry, I had to keep a tight rein on my emotions.

"You got a plan, yet?" he muttered softly, but the corners of his mouth turned up in the briefest of smiles.

Bless him for trying to break the tension. "Give me a couple of minutes, will you?" I whispered back. The ice ball released and cold resolve took over.

Going in the back door of the center was no good. You couldn't get to the rooms from either direction without using the hallway and risk being seen. The window in Byron's room wouldn't work either. No element of surprise there. Think, think—what to do?

I glanced around and the solution popped into my head.

Huge food carts—stainless steel boxes, six feet tall and about eighteen inches wide. At mealtime they were loaded with trays of food for patients. Just the thing to push along in front as a rolling shield.

I whispered for Jason to stay put a minute. A short hall angled off the back side of the lobby area and led to the center's kitchen. I darted across the Two-East opening and, moments later, found what I needed parked outside a pair of swinging doors. The doors had those porthole-style windows, but when I peeked inside, the kitchen was empty.

I opened the door and smelled stale grease and cooking odors.

A line of sweat rimmed Jason's upper lip and showed his impatience at waiting, but he smiled his approval when he saw the cart I pushed to his position. I'd found a big white apron hanging on a hook in a kitchen alcove and tied it around me. Not much in the way of camouflage, but the best I could do.

We started down the hall crouched behind our big metal shield and I prayed none of the wheels squeaked.

I glanced into a couple of rooms as we passed and saw patients in their beds, but no one looked our way. Were they asleep, unaware, or scared out of their wits?

We quickly arrived at Two-East's nurses's station and I saw two medical charts wide-open on the countertop. A coffee cup had been tipped over and coffee puddled on the counter and the floor. A set of keys dangled from the knob of a door leading to a room behind the counter, a closet with a sign reading BIO-HAZARD WASTE. A half-eaten tuna sandwich lay on the floor. Someone had stepped on it and smashed it flat.

"Ohmigod, where is everyone?" whispered Jason. "Has he killed all the nurses or what?"

"I don't know and that's a scary thought."

We crept forward silently, and when we were close enough to see it, I could tell the door to Byron's room stood open.

We stopped just short of the doorway and I pressed my ear to the wall, straining to hear. I heard only faint and distant noises; like the hum of central air, muted voices and music from radios and TVs. When I'd filtered out those, I could hear a wheezing sound coming from inside Byron's room, and that chunk of ice in my stomach grew.

Have to see, I thought. I motioned my intentions to Jason who still crouched behind the cart. I squatted into a duck-walk position hearing one of my knees crack as I did so. Hoping it wouldn't be heard by anyone inside the room, I bobbed my head around the doorjamb and jerked it back.

That quick peek, burned into my brain, showed Byron's room in semi-darkness, the blinds and curtains closed. Byron's aide, Lucy Lynn Johnstone, lay on the floor on her side facing me. That horrible wheezing sound came from her. Blood covered the chest-front of her white uniform.

Byron's bed looked empty.

"I don't see Garcia," I whispered, standing up. It took all my efforts not to scream out. "What's happened to my husband?"

"Your call."

My head jerked in an automatic response that I intended to enter the room. I slid around the doorframe moving fast—gun in hand—at the ready.

My visual survey showed an empty room, except for Lucy. Jason moved inside. He checked the bathroom while I looked in the closet. We had to make sure Garcia wasn't hiding someplace.

"Clear," said Foxx. His hushed tone still indicated his relief. "Maybe something scared him and he took off." He grunted as he knelt beside Lucy. "She's breathing." His voice came out slightly above a whisper. "I don't think her wound is serious, but it looks awful."

"What's that bastard done with my husband? And Harry? If Garcia's hurt either one . . ." My voice trailed off as my throat tightened and closed.

Women police are only suited to monitor parking meters and Austin hired several paragons of virtue in 1955. (Excerpted from: Austin History Center Records.)

Chapter 21

The muscles in my legs had turned to rubber, and for a moment, I wasn't sure if I could continue to stand. I somehow got one hand on the bed rail, just enough to steady myself until I could feel a measure of control returning to my limbs.

Jason called 911 on his cell phone to get help for Lucy.

"Take it easy, Zoe." He came over and patted my shoulder. "He can't have gone far."

"Byron can't sit in a wheelchair without being tied in it."

"Garcia probably put him on a gurney," Jason said. "This is all part of his strategy to frighten you."

"But where—?"

"Nearby, I would imagine. Didn't he say he wants to see you suffer? He wants you to witness whatever he does." He motioned towards the rear of the center. "What's in the back? Down the hall?"

"I think there's an activity room or something at the end of this hallway on one side, and maybe a lounge on the other, but—"

"That's where I'd go if I were Garcia. More room to maneuver. Don't worry, we'll find them."

Lucy Johnstone groaned, and when I turned in her direction her eyes opened and she licked her lips.

"Lucy?" I grabbed a glass and straw from the bedside table, poured some water and knelt beside her. Comprehension showed in her eyes as I put the straw in her mouth. "Here Lucy, just a tiny sip."

"Hah-ree . . ." She stammered and tried to wet her lips.

"You talked to Harry?"

She nodded, took another sip of water and tried again to speak. This time her words were clear. "He said . . ." The effort took all of her energy. She lay back, eyes closed and didn't move.

"I think Garcia's gone—but where?"

I looked down at the unconscious Lucy. "Did you call for help for her?"

Jason nodded. "EMS will be here soon. In the meantime, let's do a room check."

I hated to leave Lucy alone, but she wasn't aware and we had to find Harry and Byron.

We started with the lounge and activity rooms in back and worked our way toward the front. When we reached the Two-East nurses's desk, I stopped. Something was bugging me about this station and I had no idea why.

"Jason? You go ahead and see if you find anything."

He gave me a funny look.

"It's okay. I have a gut feeling Garcia's gone. Something happened to change his plans." Jason walked down the hallway.

Think, Zoe. Where would he go?

I sat in the swivel secretarial chair and slowly looked at everything around the station—the opened medical charts, the spilled food and those keys dangling in the doorknob of that bio-hazard waste closet. Suddenly, I remembered why I felt something was wrong with the whole picture.

One day last year, I'd gone looking for Lucy Lynn Johnstone. She was inside this little closet-sized room and a nurse was standing in the doorway. The phone rang and the nurse hurried to the desk to answer it. Lucy immediately hustled out, closed and locked the door and handed the keys to the nurse talking on the phone. The nurse, who looked sheepish, mouthed her thanks to Lucy.

"All the medications are in there," said Lucy as she and I headed towards Byron's room. "Including narcotics. It's cause for instant dismissal if the door is left unlocked."

"So you kept her out of trouble?"

"She's a good nurse and things like that can happen sometimes. Besides we look out for each other."

Now as I stared at that door I noticed the sign looked crooked and I knew that door led to a medicine closet, not a bio-hazard waste closet. I got up and inspected the sign and it fell off in my hand. Oh, shit. Someone's swapped the signs. The door was locked but the key was in the lock. I turned the key and swung the door back—fully open.

I gasped.

Austin's first experiment with using the newfangled telephone took place on December 9, 1877 . . . And Austin's first telephone exchange opened in 1881 . . . (Excerpted from: Austin History Center Records.)

Chapter 22

Byron lay on the floor on his side. On the floor over and directly under the medicine cabinet, lying in a heap, was Anthony Garcia. Blood puddled around Garcia's body. His eyes had that wide-open death stare.

As soon as I could get my heart beating again, I saw my husband's chest moving up and down, breathing rhythmically. Byron looked asleep. Thank God he was alive.

I forced my eyes to search each corner, each cabinet, every square inch, but no Harry Albright.

Bloody streaks smeared the floor, but I stepped around and between them as best I could and knelt beside my husband. Turning his head from side to side to make sure his throat was intact, I pulled his hospital gown down from his shoulders. No blood, no cuts, no stab wounds, not even a scratch that I could see. I held Byron's hand, checking him everywhere I could see, but found no injury. I breathed a sigh of relief.

When I finished with Byron, I carefully avoided the blood again and moved over to Garcia's body. I could see the gaping gunshot wound, but I felt for his carotid artery. No sign of a heartbeat.

I moved back to my husband, straightening his gown where I'd pulled it off his shoulders. I wanted to look for a blanket to cover him and a pillow for his head. I wanted to sit and hold him, but using my cell phone I woke up Lieutenant Hamilton.

"Dammit, Zoe, why didn't you tell me?" he asked whe? told him everything.

"Lieutenant, I couldn't risk Byron or Harry."

"I'm on my way out there."

"Just don't use the radio," I said. "Somehow, with Garcia dead and Hebron in the picture, things may have changed, but there's no sign of Harry here and, if Hebron has Harry's radio, he could be listening."

Hamilton had a few more choice words he scorched my eardrum with before he hung up. I sat beside Byron again, holding his hand, thinking my husband should be in bed, but I didn't want to move.

First Jason's face, then his whole body appeared in the doorway with two nurses behind him trying to look into the small room. "Oh shit," he said. "Are you okay? Is Byron okay?"

"We're fine," I said, looking at Byron who still slept. "Can't say the same for Garcia."

Jason had the saddest eyes I'd ever seen.

"The bloody mess here looks worse than it is," I said. "Did you find Harry?"

"No. I found the nursing staff—they were locked in a big pantry off the kitchen. EMS just got here and they're working on that aide," he said. "Zoe, are you sure you're okay?" He started to come inside, then realized he'd contaminate the scene and stopped.

I'd done more than enough of that already—messing up—homicide would skin me alive.

Not that I cared much. My husband's well-being was more important to me. "I'm fine. Byron's fine," I said. I wanted to cry and scream all at the same time. Anger and frustration at not finding Harry, but relief at finding Byron injured, vied for attention in my head.

Another emotion erupted without warning—guilt. Some me had longed for Byron's death. I didn't want to admit it, but it was true. His death would be the easy way out for me.

"Jason, will you please help me get Byron back in bed?" Mindful of where he stepped, Jason came in and together we lifted Byron. A nurse had located a gurney and in a few minutes we had him settled in his room. The nurse checked him thoroughly and, although they found no injuries, I insisted our doctor be called.

Jason and I went back to the nurse's station to await the crime scene personnel. I stood in the doorway looking at Tony Garcia's body. He'd shot Peppard and wanted me dead and I felt nothing. Funny, I realized that only now, in death, could I see his resemblance to Jesse Garcia, the young man I'd killed a few weeks ago. Wasted young lives. For what? An eye for an eye?

Anger had built up in me once again. "Jason, I don't know about you," I said, "but I'm going to look for Harry."

"I thought you'd never ask," he said. "Where do we look?"

"Just follow me."

In 1862, the town marshal successfully brought in a man—for a hanging—who had robbed and killed a miser. The murder weapon, a hand axe was found and through some clever sleuthing, the marshal was able to trace the evidence back to the man. The hanging took place on a temporary scaffold near the sandbank about a half-mile west of Shoal Creek. (Compiled from: Austin History Center Records.)

Chapter 23

When we walked outside, I was surprised to find it still dark, and looked at my watch—3:20. I had not been aware of time nor its passing. I drove my car and we headed north onto Dessau Road, Jason following in his van.

Until a few minutes ago, I hadn't realized how close Pecan Groves Nursing Center was to Pflugerville because I'd driven out on the interstate when I went to Hebron's trailer before. This time I took the winding back route and, in minutes, we approached the main highway leading into town. I turned left and immediately made a jog north onto the street leading to Hebron's neighborhood.

The absence of street lights after the first road made me realize how different Hebron's trailer neighborhood looked in the dark. I stopped a block away from his place and Jason, with lights already extinguished, pulled behind my car. The junk-filled, unkept lots and trailers took on a menacing air and I shivered, despite the Police windbreaker I wore.

"Where are we going?" Jason asked softly, peering into the darkness ahead.

My eyes had adjusted to the blackness and I could distinguish a few landmarks. "About a block up the street. See that row of scrub cedar trees?" He nodded. "Hebron's trailer's just beyond."

Across the street a huge dog behind a fence growled a low warning as we moved stealthily toward our destination. The dog only barked once, but that set off a chain-reaction from the other neighborhood dogs. One die-hard animal over on the next street continued as if his life depended on it. His constant barking unnerved me and I stayed in the darkest shadows I could find.

"Is anyone home?" Jason asked.

"Hard to tell from here," I said. "Have to get closer."

We moved forward, staying in the street gutters and when we were only two trailer houses away, I had a clear view of Hebron's yard, between two cedar trees. A red and white Ford pickup truck had been pulled up close to the rear end of his trailer. A faint yellow light shone in the back. I grabbed Jason's arm and spoke in a stage whisper. "That's the truck I saw the night Lianne and I got creamed. At least, it looks like the same one."

A sudden loud curse erupted from the trailer next door to our quarry and scared me out of a year's growth. We stood silently and listened. The couple's argument was muffled except for the guy's one outburst. I didn't want to get into the midst of a domestic. Fortunately, they stopped. If they started up again I wasn't sure what we'd do. Break it up? Arrest them? Ignore them? They must have given it up since we didn't hear anything else.

We had now drawn as close to Hebron's as we could without being in his lap. Suddenly Jason muttered something about a pile of dog shit along with a four-letter word or two under his breath. The smell was sickening and, in other circumstances, I might have laughed as he wiped his shoe on a piece of newspaper he found in a patch of weeds.

"We'll separate," I said, not sure I could stand his lingering doggy-do smell. "So if one of us gets caught the other can—"

"Come to the rescue?"

"Right." I tried to see if his face showed any mockery, but it was too dark to tell. "If Harry *is* a hostage, we—"

"—might need some help," Jason said. "But let's not wait for that—"

"—to happen." That's when I realized Jason and I were finishing each other's sentences. It gave me the weirdest feeling.

"Cop wavelength," he said, reading my thoughts again. "Doesn't happen often, but when it does, it's great."

"I've only heard about it. Never have experienced it."

"Me either." He glanced around quickly to see if he could spot any signs of change at the trailer. "Do you want front or back?"

"Front, I guess. Try to see inside if possible. If you see Harry, don't try anything by yourself. We'll discuss how to get him out of there. And try not to let Hebron see you. We'll make all our plans accordingly after we reconnoiter."

"Can you do bird calls or anything?" He wanted to know.

"Don't think so. Used to be able to sound like a yip-yip dog, but—"

"That'll never work." He took out his gun and started towards the backside of the trailer, using what cover he could find with the waist high weeds and two cedar trees.

I headed to the front, my gun in my left hand. I made it to the nearest corner window without much trouble and, after stubbing my toe on a cinder block, I located two more blocks and a five-gallon metal bucket. I turned the bucket upside down on top of the blocks, making a stepstool, and stepped up.

I balanced on the bucket and peered in. I couldn't see anything except a faint crack of light on the floor, underneath a closed door. I'd have to try the window on the other end.

But something blocked the second window and I couldn't see anything. The bucket creaked as if it wanted to crumple and swayed. I almost fell. I put my gun in the waistband of my Levi's in order to use both hands to step back onto the ground.

My right foot had touched dirt and immediately after my left foot stepped beside it—an arm snaked over my shoulder from behind, went around my throat—and tightened. I felt the sharp point of a knife against my right kidney.

" 'Bout time you got here, bitch. What took you so long?" Hebron's voice was harsh.

"Didn't know you were expecting me," I said.

"Garcia said you were on the way. Well, actually he said you would show up at the nursing home; I'm a little surprised to find you here."

I started to answer him, but he said, "Stop wiggling. Don't move a muscle." His arm tightened and I saw spots in front of my eyes as he squeezed.

Both my arms were free, but because of the knife I didn't dare move, except to lean into him the tiniest bit. His arm had to shift a little then to accommodate my extra body weight. That eased my breathing considerably.

His breath smelled of whiskey and stale tobacco and my stomach churned while my mind raced.

Where was Jason? Had he spotted Hebron? Was Harry somewhere inside?

I forced myself not to struggle—hoping my calmness would loosen his grip even more and it worked. "Garcia would love this," I said. "I'm sorry he's not here to see it. Did you kill him, Cowboy?"

"Asshole deserved to die. He wanted revenge so badly he almost ruined everything. All my life people ruined things. People screwed up everything for me." Cowboy shifted his weight slightly. I was keeping body pressure into him hoping he'd be a little off balance. The knife at my kidney worried me a lot, but he hadn't stuck it into flesh yet.

"Where's Harry?" I asked. "What have you done with him?"

"Dead. He tried to screw me up, too." Cowboy's voice sounded odd. His speech was slurred, like he was drunk or stoned.

Harry *dead?* That iciness crept back into my stomach. Oh no. *Harry.*

I slowly moved myself inch by microscopic inch to one side so I'd be in position to break his chokehold. "Who else really screwed you up, Cowboy? Mary Margaret?"

"Shut up! You lying bitch. Just shut up."

His arm tightened across my windpipe. A little more pressure and I wouldn't be able to breathe at all. The spots swam before my eyes again. Jason? Where was Jason?

"Guess I should tell you," he laughed. "Your redheaded buddy won't be able to help you either. He came round back stinking like dog shit or something. I took him out easy. I didn't know if he came out alone and that's when I found you."

"What did you do to him?"

He grunted, trying to shift his weight away from me. "Got to decide what to do with you, though. Could have some real fun if I wasn't in such a hurry."

Whatever drug he was on was making him crazier by the minute.

We heard a sudden noise behind us. I was so tight against Cowboy that I felt his body twitch as he tried to twist us both in order to look around. The knife eased from my kidney for a nanosecond.

Now or never, I thought, and swung my left foot out, landing it slightly behind his foot, at the same time, bringing up my left elbow to slam into his face.

Hebron didn't fall. His torso pitched back, but he was strong and I knew I hadn't done enough damage to stop him. I saw him grab his mouth with both hands, saw the blood spurt.

Everything shifted into slow motion.

"Zoe?" I heard Harry's voice. I swung my left foot again, this time aiming for Cowboy's groin. It missed, but hit his leg and I felt his knee pop.

"Zoe, I'm sooo woozy," said Harry. His voice sounded strained.

Omigosh. I got a glimpse of Harry holding a big stick as I pivoted away from Cowboy. Harry hit Cowboy in the face, then I saw Harry fall down. He landed on his backside in a semi-reclining position.

My fingers felt the reassuring grip of the Glock as I pulled it out from my waistband, business end up and ready to fire.

"Drop the knife," I said. "Or I'll blow your head off."

Cowboy's face paled in the darkness but his eyes never left mine; crazy eyes, full of hatred. I knew he wanted to lunge. Wanted to go for me. I hadn't really hurt him, but I'd slowed him down. His Navy record mentioned his expertise in the martial arts, but now the odds were completely against him and he knew it. Because I held the gun.

"You're probably thinking she won't pull the trigger," Harry said and a chuckle crept into his voice. "She's already killed one man—you want to be number two?"

Hebron laughed, but it sounded hollow. "Go ahead and shoot, bitch," Hebron said. "I don't give a crap and I can fucking guarantee you it's gonna be the last time a woman gets the best of me."

Movies played in my head on rewind and fast forward as time stopped completely. Jesse Garcia, dead on the floor of Palmer Auditorium. The sleepless nights I'd already had and the ones that would come—perhaps never ending. I wasn't sure I could pull the trigger if Cowboy came for me. Killing another human being wasn't an easy thing to do.

Then my mind movie played Tami Louise Smuts and

Mary Margaret Peppard with their throats slit. I thought of Jason Foxx somewhere behind this crummy trailer with his throat cut. I thought about what Hebron could have done to Byron. My husband didn't have much of a life and I'd probably be better off with him dead, but he did not deserve to be murdered. I thought about what this man would do to any of us if he had the chance.

Richard Cowboy Hebron wasn't a human being; he was lower than an animal. And he deserved to die.

When my mind shifted to that realization I knew I wanted to kill him. I wanted to avenge the pain he had caused. Pulling the trigger was what I'd been trained to do, what I had a license to do.

Maybe he saw that in my face. That I wanted to shoot and that I would shoot, because he suddenly dropped his arm to his side. But he didn't let go of the knife.

"Drop it," I said.

The knife thudded into the dirt. A sneer twisted his mouth. "Another time, bitch."

Jason Foxx stumbled up looking like an apparition. "Did I miss the party?"

"What did you do, stop off for coffee?"

Jason chuckled, then kept his gun on Hebron while I put handcuffs on him.

I walked to Harry still sitting on the ground and that's when I saw blood on his shirt.

"Too bad they outlawed hanging," I said. "How bad are you hurt, Harry?"

"Awww," said Harry, turning away. "He got me on the neck a little but I put on a Band-Aid and I'm fine."

Jason had also been dazed from his hit on the head but swore he'd never lost consciousness. "It just took me a few minutes to get up and get oriented again."

Jason cuffed Cowboy to his own truck's steering wheel. At Harry's instruction, Jason called headquarters to request backup and someone to transport the suspect downtown.

"I'll swear, you two look awful. Did you ask dispatch to send an ambulance?"

"Nope, we're fine," said Harry. Jason agreed and they started telling each other their version of what had happened.

While they took care of each other's egos I put my gun back into my fanny pack, walked around to the trailer's back yard and looked up at the sky. The adrenaline was subsiding, and I didn't want anyone to see my hands shake. I retched but didn't throw-up and was grateful for small favors.

I was glad I hadn't had to shoot Hebron—killing one bad guy was enough killing to last me a lifetime. But I was also relieved to know that if the situation ever came up again, I had no doubts about what I'd do.

More stars were visible here than from my mid-city apartment, and I realized how much I missed seeing the Milky Way. When I was little and when my dad wasn't too drunk, he'd point out different constellations in the night sky. I could never remember any names of anything except the Big and Little Dippers.

"And what took you so damn long to get here, Zoe?" asked Harry walking up to stand beside me.

"Maybe I'm just a little slow at solving murders, Harry."

"Is that a female thing or what?" he asked.

"Yeah, right Harry. It's all gender-related."

"Naw. You're just inexperienced. You should have called my lieutenant."

"What did you expect me to do, sit on my duff and let some guy rescue you? No way, I'm your partner. You were my responsibility."

Jason joined us and placed his arm on my shoulder. "And

a darn good partner, too."

"Damn straight," said Harry. "The best."

Jason felt nice and I leaned against him briefly before I pulled away. He smiled and I could tell he wasn't offended. Perhaps one day soon I could enjoy having someone, maybe even Jason, comfort me, but it would take time. "Thanks for all your help," I told him. "I couldn't have done it alone."

As the sirens got closer I turned to Harry. "Hey, I have to go back to the nursing home to check on my husband, but I want to hear how you doctored yourself up and got over here."

"Next time you have a few hours," Harry said, "I'll tell you all about it."

In 1855, a Travis County jail was opened. A two-story building that also housed the county courthouse. It had two-foot thick limestone walls, two courthouse rooms, a dungeon and a good jail lock. (Compiled from: Austin History Center Records: *Austin American Statesman Monthly Almanac* article.)

Chapter 24

The Emergency Room doctor put five stitches in Harry's neck and four on the bony side of his wrist. Harry hadn't known about his arm until the nurse cut off his jacket and shirt. His clothing and his arm had protected his throat and it wasn't as bad as it had looked. While being sewed up, Harry filled me in on what had happened.

"I decide to bring him in for questioning. I go by his place, but he's not there. A neighbor says Hebron's running errands in town because he's driving to Mexico tonight.

"I'm sitting in my car—Hebron's trailer staked out—when Garcia shows up out of nowhere, conks me senseless and the next thing I know, he's forcing me to drive to Pecan Groves Nursing Home. He locks up the nurses in the kitchen pantry, handcuffs me with my own cuffs, and puts me in this other closet. I'm still not tracking too well and Garcia's now got my gun and my radio.

"In a few minutes he brings your husband down there, too. I don't know what's on his mind, but I'm thinking—this's one party I'd just as soon miss."

"So what happened?" I asked.

"Garcia stayed gone; I don't know for sure how long, but a long time. When he came back, Hebron's with him and now Hebron's the one in charge. My gun is in his hand. I'm on the floor, playing possum, because by this time, I've managed to get to my handcuff key and get loose. The two had been in cahoots somehow but were feuding now. They got into an argument and Hebron just blew Garcia away. When the gun went off, I saw my chance and jumped him.

"We struggled but Hebron was damn fast with that knife. I'm sure he thought he'd killed me but I just passed out. When I came to, I'd bled like a stuck pig. Guess he thought I was dead."

"The doctor said you would have died if you hadn't put that bandage and adhesive tape on. How did you manage all by yourself?"

"Nothing to it."

"Necessity and all that," I said.

He nodded. "Afterwards I borrowed that nurse's car. She told me where her keys were. But I was weaker than I thought and had to pull off the road a couple of times to rest. When I got in his damn neighborhood, everything looked so much alike, I couldn't find Hebron's trailer. Eventually I saw you creeping around the yard with that Bozo."

"Bozo?"

"Yeah," he started laughing. "With all that bright red hair, he looks like a clown." They'd obviously given Harry something for pain and he was flying high.

"Okay, Harry. Well, your friend Bozo is now an overnight guest, too. But I told them to put you in different rooms, otherwise they'd have chaos all night."

A short time later, Harry was in his room, snoring away.

When they finished the x rays and scans on Jason's skull, I got to see him. He grumbled and complained about staying, but I promised I'd bail him and Harry both out the next day. He settled down, and although they didn't want him to sleep for a while yet, because of the concussion, he was resting when I left.

In the next few days the physical evidence against Hebron began piling up as all the reports came in. Forensics said the skin samples from Tami's fingernails, and hair samples from the motel room where Mary Margaret died, closely matched

DNA samples from Richard Hebron. The partial thumbprint also tied him to the motel. Most of Peppard's $500,000 showed up in Hebron's car.

Harry's gun had killed Garcia. Gun powder residue showed up on Hebron's hands, not Harry's. Harry didn't even remember being tested in E.R., but that didn't surprise me because he'd been doped pretty good.

The switchblade Cowboy dropped the night we'd arrested him had gone for tests at the F.B.I lab in Virginia. Slowly, Hebron's noose tightened, and the DA's case got stronger by the minute.

Hebron's attorney claimed his client had been severely abused physically and sexually as a child, but most juries have a hard time swallowing that line nowadays. We could only hope that twelve intelligent jurors would believe our story and not theirs.

The conniption fit my mother had when she learned Byron and I had been in mortal danger was short-lived. Dad's usual ploy worked and a promise for a trip to England around Christmastime got her off my back.

Avery Peppard sent me five dozen yellow roses the morning after we arrested Hebron. In appreciation, his note said. His physical prognosis was excellent but Mary Margaret's affair and death left him depressed and emotionally wrecked. Byron's Aunt Susan—the first Mrs. Peppard—was seeing him again, much to the chagrin of Byron's mother.

Luckily, Byron didn't have any repercussions from the ordeal and there still is no change in his condition. I've been talking to Doc Morton about what I should do and have decided I shouldn't see Byron so often. I can't exclude him from my life, but maybe it's time for my emotional ties to loosen slightly.

Speaking of emotions, I'm glad I didn't have to shoot

Cowboy. I've had enough on my plate dealing with the Garcia shooting. I'll continue seeing Doc until I can deal with everything. Meanwhile, I got put on desk duty again, although Harry's Lieutenant Olivera has asked me to join homicide. I'm still thinking about it.

A week after the incident at Pecan Groves, Kyle and Lianne came over for dinner, my world-famous meatloaf. I'd apologized to both of them face to face the day after Hebron's arrest.

"So what are you going to do, Zoe?" asked Kyle. He knew Harry wanted me in homicide.

Everything was cooking and we'd moved out to the deck to enjoy the day. Melody and Lyric joined us. Melody hunkered nearby and Lyric chased bugs.

"I'm not sure. You know how I like where I am, but have to admit I really enjoyed working with Harry."

"He's a great guy and an excellent cop," said Lianne. "You could learn a lot from him."

"Once you get past his prejudice against women," I said.

"He's soooo baaad." Lianne laughed and I caught Kyle looking at her with such love in his eyes it startled me. He'd left his wife and I honestly hoped things work for him and Lianne.

I felt a little jealous watching them, but the feeling didn't last long.

A voice came from the corner of the house. "Am I interrupting anything important?"

It was Jason Foxx.

"Hop over, Jason," I said.

He climbed the rail and had barely sat when Melody climbed into his lap and rubbed her head against his hand until he petted her.

The sunset turned the lake and sky all pink and golden and

I thought about how dark my life had been for over thirteen months. Maybe someday soon I'd be able to let light back into my world.

Later, after we'd eaten, someone suggested we go to Dance Across Texas. "Only if you call a taxi to drive us there and back," said Lianne. "I'm not riding with anyone who's drinking."

We all agreed and we also agreed on coffee and dessert first.

Lianne and Jason began a heavy discussion when I went inside to make the coffee. As I brought out plates for chocolate cake, Lianne grabbed my hand and pulled me back into the kitchen.

"I like Jason," she said.

"I do, too," I said. "But I'm taking this slow. It's not easy to move away from my feelings for Byron."

Before she could voice her opinion, the phone rang and I picked up the receiver.

"Zoe, you ready to rock and roll?"

"Harry? What in the world are you talking about?"

"We just got a double murder out near Zilker Park. I'll pick you up in fifteen minutes."

"I'm not a homicide detective," I said.

"No, but if you keep practicing you will be," he said, breaking the connection.

The thrill kicked in and the adrenaline pumped. I turned to my guests. "Sorry. Guess I'll have to take a rain check on the rest of the evening." Three faces looked at me in astonishment.

"That was Harry," I said.

"She has to go," said Jason, softly. "Austin City blue runs through her veins."